THE PEOPLE IN THE PICTURE

THE PEOPLE IN THE PICTURE

HAYDN MIDDLETON

BALLANTINE BOOKS • NEW YORK

The passages on pages vii and 255 are taken from *The Tale of Taliesin*
and *The Battle of the Trees*. They were translated from the original Welsh
by Lady Charlotte Guest and D. W. Nash.

Library of Congress Cataloging-in-Publication Data

Middleton, Haydn.
  The people in the picture.

  I. Title.
PR6063.I248P46 1988   823'.914   87-91362
ISBN 0-345-34728-5

Text design by Holly Johnson
Manufactured in the United States of America

First American Edition: May 1988
10 9 8 7 6 5 4 3 2

For Fiona, with love

Primary chief bard am I to Elphin,
And my original country is the region of the summer stars;
Idno and Heinin called me Merddin,
At length every king will call me Taliesin . . .
I have been teacher to all intelligences,
I am able to instruct the whole universe.
I shall be until the day of doom on the face of the Earth;
And it is not known whether my body is flesh or fish.

THE
PEOPLE
IN THE
PICTURE

1

IT WAS JASMIN WHO MADE THE FIRST MOVE, NOT LACY. THAT was the awkward but undeniable truth.

Regardless of everything that happened afterward, it was Jasmin who made the first move. If she hadn't called out to him, late on that summer afternoon, he would probably have walked straight past. He hadn't given her any kind of encouragement. He hadn't even been looking in her direction.

There was no escaping the fact that Jasmin was the one who started it. Sitting up there on her knoll in the park, she quite simply summoned Lacy into her life.

And Lacy, of course, didn't have to be asked twice.

JASMIN WAS IN THE PARK THAT SATURDAY ONLY BY chance. The boys and their friends had commandeered the small back lawn for croquet. So she'd taken her book to the park instead. She walked halfway up the incline and sat down on the top of a little unkempt knoll. Beneath her the city seemed to sparkle in the low sunlight. Somewhere behind her an English Civil War society was reenacting a battle.

The sun was still hot. Jasmin was glad she'd worn her sundress. At thirty-three she looked good—supple and slim, with perpetually fawn-colored skin and short, dark hair. Several men had told her that she was beautiful but she hadn't let it go to her head. (She'd grown up alongside a far prettier younger sister. As a result she'd always regarded her own body as a kind of liability.)

She read right through to the end of her book—a light romantic novel—oblivious to the smoke and din of the mock battle. The novel left her feeling pensive, well-disposed, better than she'd felt for some weeks. There was no reason to go back to the house at once. So she pulled her knees up to her chin, linked her fingers across her shins, and stared down at the city for almost half an hour.

She heard the chinking of his unfastened belt buckles before she saw him. He was one of the soldiers, a Cavalier in a plumed hat, skirting the base of the knoll and heading toward the main gate. His head was down. There was every possibility that he hadn't even noticed her. Every possibility.

Hello, Jasmin called down to him brightly. Are you a deserter?

Thus it was Jasmin who made the first move. (This in itself wouldn't have surprised those who knew her well. She'd opened conversations with plenty of strange men in her time. On platforms, in pubs, in waiting rooms. Some girls like to talk, some don't. That was just the way Jasmin happened to be.)

The soldier stopped and squinted up at her. In one hand he held a sword, in the other a can of lager. He was five or six feet beneath her. Jasmin judged him to be twenty-six, twenty-seven. Certainly younger than herself. His face was round, puckered and red like a colicky baby's.

No, he told her, I'm not deserting. I've got to get away and put my kids to bed. Tell them a story, you know?

He leaned on his sword as if it were a walking stick, crossed his ankles, and took a long draught of lager. Then he planted the empty can on the grass and looked about him. Marvelous here, isn't it? he said.

Lovely, said Jasmin.

Marvelous.

He rummaged in his huge jacket pocket and pulled out a brown paper bag. He held it up to her. Can I offer you a pear? he said. They're British.

No thanks, laughed Jasmin.

He took one himself. He ate it quickly, holding it like a chicken drumstick, then he carefully placed the core on top of the lager can. Again he surveyed the cityscape below. Marvelous, he repeated, Absolutely marvelous. And, without more ado, he began to talk Jasmin through his afternoon on the battlefield.

Jasmin soon stopped paying close attention to what he was saying. He was clearly very drunk indeed. His intonation seemed odd, too. Eventually she identified a Welsh accent, fading in and out of his discourse like a rogue radio signal. Twice more he mentioned his kids.

So Jasmin not only made the first move. From the very beginning she had good reason to believe that he was married, settled down—and therefore unfair game. This only made the immediate developments in their relationship so much more perplexing.

He fell silent, then with one hand he removed his hat and scratched his head. Jasmin blinked. Fortunately the soldier was too far away to hear her little gasp of astonishment. His head was completely shaven. From where Jasmin was sitting it looked like a well-thumbed dome of modelling clay. And somehow the baldness made his face seem younger, rawer.

Jasmin raised herself to her feet. I shall have to be getting back, she said, smoothing down her dress.

The soldier dumped the hat back on his head. He reached out a hand to help her down the knoll. She smiled at him but descended without his assistance.

They headed for the main gate side by side. Along the way he chattered animatedly about whatever caught his fancy. Spiders, cricket, topography, the stars. Again he offered her a pear. Again she declined and again he swiftly munched through one himself.

Jasmin's house was less than five minutes walk from the park. When she arrived there, the garrulous soldier was still at her side. My God, he said, staring up at the big Edwardian villa, My God, is this all yours?

Jasmin chuckled. I wish it was. No, I share it. With four others.

She wondered whether to mention that the four others were all men, and immediately decided against it. She could look after herself. She always had in the past. It was one of her last remaining sources of pride. So the soldier followed her in through the side entrance, for all the world as if she had invited him back for the coffee and cake which she finally felt obliged to set before him.

While he ate and drank, without removing his hat, Jasmin moved restlessly about the large kitchen. She'd noticed on entering the house that the boys were no longer out on the lawn. They would almost certainly have gone along to the pub. So she was on her own, possibly for the rest of the evening.

I like your outfit, she said breezily to the soldier. (It looked authentic, expensive.)

Ah, he said, his mouth full, I borrowed it, my love. For the day, like. I'm not what you'd call a regular soldier.

Then he began to talk distractedly about trees and shrubs. In the course of this, apropos of nothing, he informed Jasmin that he was a scaffolder. Jasmin sat down opposite him and propped her chin on her hands. She couldn't help being amused. The men with whom she usually mixed were a tentative, inhibited lot. This solder, although quite possibly simple in the head, paraded his knowledge with such relish, such zest.

What about your kids? she said to him during a lull in his sequence of monologues. Won't you be terribly late?

Kids? he asked her back, his face dulled by bewilderment. And it was then that the phone rang.

There was a phone in the kitchen. But Jasmin chose to take the call upstairs, on the extension in her room. (She was expecting to hear from an old friend, a man, who'd told her that he was hoping to be in the city for the weekend.) She made her excuses and left the soldier at the kitchen table.

The phone was on a small occasional table beside the bed.

Jasmin! (It was a woman's voice, reedy, apprehensive.) Thank God you're all right!

Jasmin sighed through her nose. Eileen, she said, What is it?

There was a pause at the other end. Eileen was Jasmin's mother. She lived with Jasmin's retired father in a town eighty miles to the south and she spoke with her elder daughter four or five times every week.

I know you'll say I'm ridiculous, Eileen began, But I was having a nap just now and I had this vile dream. Oh God, Jas! All of you were in it, all of you. I know these dreams. Like a warning it was. Like a warning that something godawful's going to happen . . .

Eileen listen, Jasmin interrupted, Can I ring you later?

I've got someone here now. I'll ring you later and you can tell me all about it. Is that all right?

Yes . . . yes. She sounded badly shaken. In most ways she was a competent, sensible woman. But she'd always set enormous store by horoscopes, dreams, otherworldly intimations. Jasmin reasoned with her briefly then replaced the receiver. She stood for a moment at her window, looking down into the next-door garden. A little mulatto girl was pedaling back and forth furiously on a red bicycle.

When she turned to leave the room she found the soldier blocking the doorway. His head was bare.

I didn't hear you come up, she said. Her legs began to tingle.

Anything important? he asked, his shoulder wedged tight against the doorframe.

Sorry?

He nodded sharply at the phone. Anything important?

Oh. No. Nothing important.

The soldier pushed himself off the doorframe and stepped into the room. One of the house cats followed him in. It swarmed around his great leather boots. The soldier looked down, made a clucking noise with his mouth. Then he stepped forward and in one stride he virtually crossed the room. He was close enough now for Jasmin to smell his breath. Pears, coffee, no alcohol. He seemed completely sober.

He raised his hand. Jasmin's eyes widened. He was pointing at the bulletin board on the wall above the phone. It was smothered with postcards, scrawled-on pieces of paper, numbers, addresses, old messages. There was also a single photograph.

Is that your family? he asked.

She nodded, peering at the photo as if she too were

seeing it for the first time. She felt extremely unsteady. The soldier's hand was huge but smooth. Not like a manual worker's hand at all. Not like a scaffolder's hand. Nothing like her own father's hand.

Tell me about your family, he said coaxingly. Go on, tell me all about them.

For all her unsteadiness, Jasmin frowned at him. He seemed perfectly serious. Genial now, yet perfectly serious. Entirely different from the way he'd been in the kitchen. And he seemed bulkier in the dimness of the room, short of six feet but stocky, substantial. Yet the greatest alteration of all was in his face.

Jasmin had never seen anything like it. In his eye sockets, and between his parted lips, there was now an alarming opacity. Jasmin would have sworn that it was more than just a trick of the light. It was as if a shadow had somehow insinuated itself right inside his head.

There was a sudden metallic crash in the garden next door. Jasmin started. She looked out of the window and saw that the little girl had fallen off her bicycle. Already her screams were shattering the evening calm.

You really want to know about my family? asked Jasmin, turning back to the photo.

Really, the soldier replied, clasping his hands behind his back. He began to rock back and forth on the balls of his feet. The cat continued to lavish attention on him.

Jasmin leaned across him and switched on the bedside lamp. She directed its light at the bulletin board, then introduced him to her assembled relatives. She talked haltingly, perfunctorily. It was a long time since she'd talked to anyone about her parents, her sister, her great-aunt. She'd long ago stopped trying to explain why they had such a distressing effect on her. But she worked her way through them all. Everyone, that was, except herself.

The soldier leaned forward, resting his forearm along the wall above the cork runner, and peered even closer at the picture.

Then there's you, my love, he said. What's your name?

Jasmin. Jasmin Piast. What's yours?

He didn't appear to hear her question. Piast, he said. What's that? Not English?

It's Polish, Jasmin told him. My father's Polish. He . . . he came here after the war.

The soldier ran his tongue along his top lip. His eyes had narrowed to the blackest of slits. He seemed to be almost entranced, rooted to the floorboards, to all intents and purposes assimilating the information that Jasmin had given him. She took the opportunity to step briskly aside.

You look like good people, he said at last.

We're just ordinary, Jasmin replied, stepping back into the openness of the room. There are thousands of families like ours. Millions. There's nothing very special about us.

The soldier slowly shook his head. Jasmin didn't consider, at that stage, that he was genuinely interested in her family. Moment by moment she was expecting him to turn and lay his hands on her. Those big pulpy hands. She pressed a couple of buttons on her music center. A conversation between two women was being broadcast on the local radio station.

What's your name? she asked him again.

Lacy, he said, without taking his eyes from the photograph. Terence Lacy. But I'm known by many names. All things to all people, that's me.

Jasmin laughed, but when at length Lacy turned to face her he wasn't smiling himself. He looked exhausted, utterly discomposed, and old. He seemed to have aged by a full ten years since Jasmin had looked him over from the top of her knoll in the park. But as he gazed at her the shadow was slinking back inside the depths of his head. His eyes were resurfacing in the pale lamplight. He nodded apologetically.

I'm taking up your time, he said. I must let you get on with your life.

He followed Jasmin out on to the landing and down the stairs. The atmosphere in the house seemed eerily oppressive. It was as if, just moments before, all the rooms had been filled with contentious voices.

Piast, he said on the way down the stairs. I like the sound of that.

It was the name of a Polish royal family once, said Jasmin. Hundreds of years ago.

Aha. Then you're a princess.

Jasmin smiled.

I expect you're booked up this evening? Lacy asked her in the hall. The cat had come down with him and was continuing to nuzzle his boots.

As a matter of fact I am, Jasmin lied, opening the front door for him. He was on his way down the steps when Jasmin remembered that his sword and hat were still in the kitchen. She went to fetch them, and on receiving them from her Lacy clicked his heels and gave a little bow. Had he left them behind on purpose? Had he wanted an excuse to come back? It was impossible to tell from the look in his eyes.

I'll see you around then, she said.

And he saluted, and swaggered off down the street with the weapon over his shoulder. As Jasmin shut herself back inside, she saw him fishing in his cavernous pocket again for the bag of pears.

She went straight back up to her room. Quite unaccountably she was beginning to quake. She directed the lamplight away from the bulletin board, closed the curtains and went down to the kitchen to cook herself a simple supper.

An hour or so later, as she was shifting some crockery from the draining board, her hands started to tremble violently. She dropped and smashed a Pyrex bowl, and had to sit clutching the end of the table until the tremors subsided.

When she'd cleared up the mess she returned to her room, nauseous and alarmed. She stumbled across to the bulletin board. Crazy as it seemed, she half expected to find her relatives' images wiped clean from the photo. Completely expunged.

The images were still there though. Nothing had changed. But for the rest of that evening she couldn't shake off the notion that she'd somehow betrayed her family. Delivered their souls into the hands of a stranger.

This wasn't entirely out of character. When it came to her family, Jasmin had always tended toward the melodramatic. Her relationships with her sister and her parents were based on bitter, unresolved antagonism. Even though she'd spent half her life outside the family home, she'd never been able to distance herself from the old quarrels and furies and rivalries.

By ten-thirty it was obvious that her man friend wasn't going to ring. Jasmin didn't mind. (She'd taught herself to be socially adaptable. She'd had to be. Most of her friends had many more commitments than herself.) With no great enthusiasm she finally rang her mother.

Eileen hadn't got over her dream. Tetchily she refused to describe it now to Jasmin. I know you don't believe in any of it, she said. I don't see why I should give you a damn good laugh. So Eileen talked instead about an old schoolfriend of Jasmin's, a girl who had recently given birth to her third child. Jasmin listened patiently. She listened to her mother's words and she listened to the current of accusation that ran beneath them. And they reached the end of their conversation without actually falling out.

Jasmin lay awake for a long time before drifting off to sleep. *A warning*, Eileen had said to her earlier, when the shaven-headed soldier had been making his way up her stairs, *A warning that something godawful's going to happen . . .* Jasmin didn't at that point connect the premonition with Terence Lacy. But she had a shrewd idea that she hadn't seen the last of him. He'd left too much of a mark on the house (and on her) to stay away.

Yet she didn't expect him to reappear as soon as he did— just before twelve-thirty on the following morning.

3

JASMIN WAS READING IN THE BACK GARDEN WHEN LACY knocked at the door. One of the boys answered and told him to go straight through.

I'd like you to accept these, he said, presenting Jasmin with a bunch of at least fifty carnations.

Jasmin, stunned and delighted, took them. It was a long time since anyone had given her flowers.

I got them outside the hospital, like, he explained shyly. He was still wearing the Cavalier uniform, and gave every appearance of having slept in it.

Jasmin thanked him, laughing incredulously. She knew that the boys were watching from the kitchen window. I haven't got a vase big enough for them all, she said. I'll have to split them up. Come inside. Please.

While Jasmin fussed with the flowers, Lacy sat at the kitchen table and chatted good-naturedly with the boys. Jasmin was too disorientated to listen closely. Cars, they were talking about. Makes of car and brands of beer.

There! She indicated the three full vases on the draining board. They look gorgeous. I'll take them up to my room.

Oh, don't go disappearing, love, said Lacy. I wondered if you'd care for a drink down the street? Just a quick one, like.

The boys all looked at Jasmin. She could hardly have refused him. Yes all right, she said. That would be nice.

They walked under the hot sun to a main-road pub close to the park entrance. Lacy's exuberance of the previous evening seemed to have disappeared. When he talked, as inconsequentially as ever, he looked haggard, forbidding. Perhaps it was because he hadn't shaved. Yet even his voice sounded different. It was as if somebody else was wearing his body.

Did you get back in time to put your kids to bed? Jasmin asked, wondering what his wife had thought about him staying out all night.

Lacy didn't answer immediately. Then he simply grinned at her, raised his eyebrows, and rolled his eyes. Jasmin smiled back, too much taken aback to press him any further. He slapped his pocket and cursed. Do you know, he said to her grimly, I'm completely out of pears.

The pub was dark and full of smoke. It wasn't a place that Jasmin herself would have chosen for a drink. A group of young men and women whistled at Lacy from the bar. They turned out to be people he knew.

16

This is Miss Jasmin Piast, he announced to them. I am right, my love, am I? It is "Miss"?

Jasmin nodded.

Miss Piast is a Polish princess living in exile, said Lacy.

Jasmin took scant notice as Lacy identified his eight or nine friends for her. She hadn't been expecting a party. (But then, she wondered later, what exactly *had* she been expecting?) Some of them were very young indeed, eighteen or nineteen. They were all what Eileen would have called common. None of them seemed at all surprised that Lacy should still be wearing his fancy dress.

The next hour or so wasn't remarkably enjoyable. Lacy bought her a gin-and-tonic. He remained at her side. But he seemed far more interested in the others than in talking to her. Their conversations, which revolved entirely around sport and the previous day's battle, were impersonal, even formal. It was almost, Jasmin felt, as if they had been scripted in advance.

One of the boys bought a fresh round of drinks. That's some sword of old Lacy's, eh? he said, smiling at Jasmin as he handed her another gin. The girls giggled. Someone made another, plainly ribald, remark which Jasmin didn't quite catch.

She flushed, grinned, and tried to suppress some unpleasant speculations of her own. (Had Lacy perhaps fetched her from the house as a kind of bet? Had he been spinning these people a ripe story about the night before and then been dared to go and get her?) Jasmin gazed at the racing prints on the walls. It didn't bear thinking about. Really it didn't.

Do you work? a squat boy in a cricket pullover suddenly asked her.

Well yes I do, she replied. But as from tomorrow I'm taking a sort of extended break from it.

Between jobs, eh?

No, she countered, mildly affronted. I work for myself. I'm an illustrator. There's plenty of work if I want it. Too much really. I've just decided to take the summer off, that's all.

Must be very nice, said the squat boy. If you can afford it.

Oh, I don't know, said Lacy, who hadn't appeared to be listening up to that point. He looked Jasmin in the eye. I'd always take the work if it was there, he went on. It doesn't do to fester now, does it?

Fester! The nerve of the man! Jasmin sipped her drink. She knew that anything she said would sound either prim or arch. So she said nothing at all, and Lacy once again turned his attentions elsewhere.

Eventually she went to the bar herself and bought Lacy a beer. He had after all bought her the carnations.

Thank you kindly, Miss Piast, he said, taking the glass. And what will you be doing with yourself for the rest of this fine day? (The intake of alcohol seemed to be perking him up again.)

I'm going to someone's for lunch. Jasmin told him. It was the second time she'd fabricated a social engagement to put him off. In fact I really should be going now.

You see your people a lot, do you? he asked, disregarding what she'd said.

I'm sorry?

Your folks, you know. Your family. Do you get together often?

What a peculiar question, thought Jasmin, smiling weakly. No. No not really. My sister lives abroad. We haven't been together as a family since that photo was taken. Two or three years, I suppose.

Abruptly she stopped speaking, wondering why on earth she was furnishing him with this kind of detail. He noticed her unease and laughed.

So it takes something out of the ordinary to bring you all together, then?

Jasmin bit her lip. You could say that, yes.

Well, I must say I liked the look of them. Good people. Good people . . .

He was beginning to get on Jasmin's nerves. She wished she hadn't come out with him. She wished she hadn't drunk two gins on top of an empty stomach. She wished that she really *had* been invited to a lunch party, where she could mix with her own sort of people and talk with quiet humor about her shaven-headed Cavalier.

She looked at her watch. I must dash, she said. I'm awfully late. Thanks again for the flowers. They were lovely, really lovely. I'll see you.

Lacy nodded, then cocked his head and stared at her as she made for the door. Back in the sunlight, Jasmin felt as if she'd been reprieved. But from what, exactly, she wasn't able to say.

She walked home by a roundabout route. Almost immediately her attitude to Lacy began to soften. It was quite possible that he hadn't been ignoring her on purpose in the pub. It was even feasible that he'd felt nervous in her company. She regretted that she'd left him so gracelessly. He'd really done nothing to deserve it. In spite of the peculiar things he'd said to her, he'd really done nothing to deserve it.

Her mild interest in him, she assured herself, had nothing to do with sex. She found him physically antipathetic,

19

and, besides, he was almost certainly married. No, Terence Lacy hadn't been her kind of man. But she was sorry to think that she might never see him again, sorry that she'd written him off quite so readily. There was, after all, plenty of space in her life for someone a little bit left of center.

When she got back to her house she made some tea and toast and took it up to her room. She raised her mug in mock salute to the photo of her family, the photo that had entranced Lacy. *So it takes something out of the ordinary to bring you all together?* That's what he'd said. And then he'd looked at her in such an oddly confidential way. A look which had suggested that it was well within his own powers to orchestrate a family reunion.

Ah well, thought Jasmin. Ah well.

4

DURING THE TWO WEEKS THAT FOLLOWED, JASMIN TRIED TO get herself into a holiday mood. She read some undemanding books, sunbathed in the garden, went swimming in the river. Twice she drove her Deux Chevaux into the country and found peaceful places to walk. In the evenings she drank at pavement tables with friends, or ate alone in unpretentious restaurants.

But with each day she grew more and more uneasy. She didn't feel guilty about not working. It wasn't that at all, although her agent was giving her a pretty hard time. (He'd said he was going to send her the typescript of a mythological story. He wanted her to read it and rough out some sample illustrations within two weeks.) Jasmin was disturbed rather by the untidiness of her life, its persistent lack of shape or definition. As a rule she was quite optimistic, but now she couldn't help feeling unfulfilled in every province of her life that she considered important.

Her most immediate reason for regret was the house. She'd been hoping to have it to herself over the summer. But almost at once she'd had to rethink her plans, because three of the four boys chose to stay on through their vacation.

The boys were students of estate management, coltish and superficially charming but not really all that bright. Jasmin had been renting rooms with similar people ever since she'd left home for art school. In some ways it was preferable to living alone. It was nice to have someone to answer the phone when she was out. It was good not to have to feel frightened in the night. But she'd been looking forward enthusiastically to having some privacy over the summer.

Before the fourth boy disappeared for his tour of southern Europe, Jasmin asked if she could store her working materials in his room. He told her to feel free. Once he was gone, the other three helped her to shift her easels, worktop, and stool down the landing. She felt better about her room now that it didn't have to double as a studio. She filled the empty spaces with potted plants. The cats began to come in more often to sleep on the uncovered floorboards.

Yet the sense of unease wouldn't leave her. And as was usually the way, she made herself feel a lot worse by talking regularly on the phone with Eileen. Once or twice in the course of these conversations she mentioned Terence Lacy. She confided in her mother about all her men. She always had. Her confidences had come to compensate, in some small way, for the fact that she still wasn't married.

Eileen was arrested by the idea of Lacy's shaven head. But she obviously considered a scaffolder a poor bargain for her talented daughter. Jasmin told her that he had children; she tried to stress that her own interest in him was purely Platonic. It did no good. Eileen interpreted each episode in Jasmin's life as a maneuver to secure a partner. Such conflicts of opinion had been a source of ill will between them for as long as either could remember.

Jasmin knew that she was a disappointment to her parents. The knowledge could still prostrate her with remorse. Her father, who had anglicized his Polish name to Sidney, had little interest in her as an individual. Unlike Eileen he didn't yearn for a son-in-law or a series of grandchildren. But he'd badly wanted Jasmin to succeed as an artist. And— to be blunt about it—she'd let him down.

As a girl she'd bristled with accomplishments. She'd then failed to realize her full potential at art school. But in the long years that followed she'd worked hard at her portraiture, while making a reasonable living from free-lance book design, bits and pieces of advertising work, and, recently, book illustration.

Her agent believed in her fiercely, almost as fiercely as Sidney himself. He'd presented her with an embarrassment of opportunities to better herself. But somehow the big commissions had never come her way. She painted competently, often imaginatively. But there were a lot of good people around. And Jasmin just didn't seem to have the wherewithal to set herself apart from the rest.

It was after coming face to face with this truth that Jasmin had decided to stop working for the duration of her thirty-fourth summer. To those who were interested, she described this break, wryly, as a "sabbatical season." Wryly, because the phrase sounded rather grand for a humble illustrator. (Similar self-consciousness, coupled with honesty, had long since stopped her from calling herself an artist.)

She didn't have a great deal of money to finance herself through this sabbatical season. She tended to spend most of her income as she earned it. But she'd saved enough to get by for a couple of months. All she wanted now was time to think. Time to read and time to stay calm. When her friends suggested that she might be trying to "find herself" she laughed politely. When they hinted that "a new man" might point her in the right direction, she became quite touchy.

As a collection, Jasmin's friends mattered to her greatly but they weren't ideal. Most of them were married. Some of them, more irksomely, had been married and were now single parents. Too many of them by far were Jasmin's former lovers.

These lovers were all much of a muchness. Down-at-heel professional types, usually amusing, sometimes cynical, always thoroughly decent. The sort of men who often got things wrong and didn't mind apologizing. Anodyne men. Men whom she knew her father would despise.

Yet Jasmin had devoted a lot of care and attention to her relationships. Each liaison began with the measured stateliness of a pavane. Jasmin liked it that way. She liked to watch the new man adjusting his previous patterns, reforming his old timetables, drawing away from his former commitments. She took comfort from the gentle development of confidence, the familiar process of compromise, admission, and, eventually, protestation.

But she was far too cautious ever to overreach herself. Unconsciously in part, she had worked out an extremely conservative code of conduct for herself. She'd always opted for safe men. (Men who respected her independent spirit and didn't have the verve or courage to threaten it. And it was always Jasmin who broke off with them, not vice versa.) She'd had proposals. Three different men had proposed to her. She supposed that one day she would marry one of these types. But somehow she'd never been able to accept any single one of them.

So it was easy to stay friendly with her ex-lovers. Easy, that is, up to a point. Jasmin knew that it was civilized to eat dinners cooked by these men's wives—but she also found it vaguely ignoble. She enjoyed giving presents on their children's birthdays—but even that made her feel like a charlatan.

The children were vitally important, of course. Very few of her friends didn't have them. She moved in a world of toddlers and babysitters and bag-eyed, shouting parents. She didn't really resent this. In a way she was jealous, and longed to have a family of her own. But she felt taxed by the sheer relentlessness of other people's offspring. She sometimes wished that they didn't have to be quite so central. (It was rather appropriate, she thought later, that Lacy's first remarks to her should have been about children.)

One evening, waiting for her coffee in a little trattoria, it occurred to her that she had no need at all to "find herself." She knew exactly where she was, where she'd steered herself. She was nowhere.

Everything about her was indeterminate. In her work she was neither a success nor a complete failure. She was no longer young but not yet middle-aged. She was still undecided as to whether she should stay single or commit herself to a partner. When it came to a sense of nationality she didn't feel completely English, yet she certainly didn't think of herself as Polish. She wasn't even sure whether, sentimentally, she thought herself working class or bourgeois.

I'm in the twilight zone, she told herself, feeling all the more jaded because she couldn't see any immediate route out of it.

When she got home that evening the boys and a couple of girls were playing cards in the kitchen.

Your friend called this evening, one of them said as Jasmin passed through.

Which friend?

The bald guy. The one who brought the flowers.

Jasmin paused. Did he say what he wanted?

No. There was no message. He waited for a bit and then he went.

Jasmin was sorry that she'd missed him. Ah well, she thought again. Ah well.

Climbing the stairs, she saw that the door to her room, which she'd closed on her way out, was now slightly ajar. This disconcerted her. Surely the boys hadn't let Lacy wait for her in there? She pushed the door open and scanned the room. The marmalade cat was curled up asleep on the bed. Everything else was just as she'd left it.

Instinctively her eyes fell on the photo of her family. Nothing, as far as she could see, had been touched. But again she sensed a kind of diminishing echo in the room. Not of people shouting this time. It was smoother than that now. More like singing—a chorus of male voices perhaps.

She threw her bag on to the bed and went back down to the kitchen.

You didn't let my friend wait in my room, did you? she asked.

No, said one of the girls, He sat in here with us. Oh, he did go up to the loo though? Why?

No reason, said Jasmin. It's not important.

And first thing the next day, Lacy came back.

5

HE CAME IN A CHERRY RED ESCORT, JUST AFTER BREAKFAST ON that Saturday morning. Jasmin was in the living room and saw him pulling up.

Look, he said as soon as she opened the front door to him. Why don't you be a devil? I've booked a couple of rooms for tonight at a hotel in St. David's.

St. David's? What, in Wales? Jasmin's head immediately swam with unworthy thoughts. She felt sure that some girl-friend must have let him down at the last moment.

St. David's in the ancient land of Dyfed, he confirmed. Right on the edge, where the land meets the sea. And if I were you, love, I'd bring a good strong waterproof. There's nowhere on earth like it for rain.

Jasmin smiled at him. It was the first time she'd seen him in contemporary dress. There was a red knit hat on his head, and he was wearing a black singlet and shorts, with brand new training shoes on his feet. In fact the entire outfit looked new. Jasmin could still see the creases where the singlet and shorts had been folded.

He began to jog on the spot, throwing pretend punches and blushing at her. His body was plaster white but he looked good in a muscular sort of way. He also seemed taller, more broad-shouldered than Jasmin remembered.

Why St. David's? she asked.

Whyever not? he asked back, shrugging, turning his palms upwards and jogging faster. (*Rooms,* he'd said. *A couple of rooms.*)

What would we do there?

Whatever you like. Eat a bit, drink a bit. See what there is to see. Oh, come on, why don't you give it a go?

Jasmin bowed her head. She couldn't make herself think clearly. Already she knew that she was going to go with him. She badly needed a change. And she'd had enough of inventing a social calendar to put him off. All right, so he was probably married. That was his business.

Come in, she said. I'll have to throw a few things in a bag.

She liked the way that sounded. She felt like a girl in a Swinging Sixties film. Lacy followed her up the stairs, rubbing his hands together purposefully and chattering on about the weather forecast. He watched from her bedroom doorway as she packed a few essentials and scribbled a note to the boys.

You came last night? she said.

Oh, right. I was just passing, like.

I . . . I'm sorry I missed you.

28

She couldn't bring herself to ask him if he had come into her room. Not now. Why on earth should he have, after all? It had probably just been one of the boys. They sometimes came in to borrow her records or wine glasses when she was out. Anyway, it didn't matter to her now. Not now.

I see the old carnations have had it, said Lacy, nodding at the nearest vaseful. (They'd all died within a couple of days. Jasmin didn't know how to keep flowers alive. Neither did she know when to throw them away.)

Oh, I am sorry, she said. I've never been much good with flowers.

Ah, there we are, he said airily. You haven't had enough practice probably.

Jasmin shrugged at him. (She found it very hard to keep her wits about her when she was with Lacy. It was only later that she realized how rude his remark had been. Rude, and yet accurate, too, like so many of the things he was going to say to her.)

You can bring some of those cassettes for the car if you like, he told her. Jasmin picked up half-a-dozen tapes and thrust them into his hand. She let him carry her canvas bag down the stairs and out to the car. Jasmin found him rather gallant, even if he did look extraordinary in his knit hat and running gear. There was an unusual innocence about him. This innocence wasn't to be confused, Jasmin now realized, with simple-mindedness.

She had no idea what she was letting herself in for as she struggled to fasten her seat belt. She wasn't altogether sure that she cared. Lacy waited patiently for a break in the traffic so that he could do a three-point turn. Jasmin's next door neighbor, a frail-looking man of over seventy, was standing at his gate. He waved.

Lacy reached across Jasmin and pulled a brown paper bag from the glove compartment. He dropped it into her lap.

There, he said. Hazelnuts. There's a nutcracker at your feet. You just eat as many as you like. I'll have the odd one. When it suits you, like.

He began to swing the car around. Jasmin frowned at him. She couldn't tell from his expression whether he was sending her up. I'm sorry, she said, I'm not all that fond of nuts.

Oh, there's a pity, he replied. They're special, you see, hazelnuts are. (He was still performing his three-point turn as he spoke.) They're good for the brain, they give you wisdom.

Is that so? said Jasmin. Would you like one now?

No, no, my love. I'm fine at the moment . . .

Then, after Lacy had driven no more than thirty yards up the street, Jasmin made him stop the car. She did so with a short involuntary cry which surprised herself as much as it surprised him. Lacy turned to her. Hey, steady on now, he said, What's the problem?

Jasmin had no immediate answer. She didn't know for the life of her why she'd cried out. I've forgotten something, she told him, just to cover herself.

Lacy nodded and reversed straight back down the busy street. Then he waited behind the wheel while Jasmin re-entered her house, climbed the stairs and opened the door to her room. She was trembling all over. She had to sit on the end of the bed to gather herself. This was just how she'd been on that evening after meeting Lacy in the park. The room was ringing all around her. Her gaze swept across the furniture, the dead flowers, the books, the records. The shouts of the little girl next door were spiraling up and in through the window which Jasmin had left open.

I'm in bad shape, she told herself, seriously bad shape. She put a hand to her throat and closed her eyes. The palpitations were slowing down. I shouldn't be like this, she thought. This isn't the way I ought to be at all.

She stood, walked across to the window and closed it. And in a virtual continuation of the downward movement, she pulled the photo of her family from the bulletin board and slipped it into her shoulder bag.

Something important? Lacy asked as she belted herself in again.

Well no, not really, said Jasmin, smiling and patting her shoulder bag. But she was lying again.

6

JASMIN HAD NEVER BEEN ABLE TO LEAVE HER FAMILY BEHIND.
That was the most profound and continuous of all her
problems.

The Piast family wasn't a happy one. Jasmin, Kate, Sidney, and Eileen had never really been able to get along with
one another. The causes of the acrimony could be trivial
yet at the same time deeply embedded in the history of the
household.

Their plight seemed to be summed up in the photo
which was now inside Jasmin's shoulder bag. No one before
Lacy had ever remarked on that photo. Unwittingly he had

honed in on the focal point of the room. That, at least, was the way Jasmin saw it.

The photo was a joke item, a color snapshot that had gone unintentionally wrong. It had been taken three summers before, when Jasmin's great uncle and aunt had been celebrating their sixtieth wedding anniversary. (The last time, as she'd told Lacy, that the family had been together.) Eileen had organized a tea-and-sandwiches party in the old couple's little garden. Late in the afternoon, old Frank, Jasmin's great uncle, had insisted on taking a snapshot of the four Piasts.

Old Frank had been a camera buff for years. But at eighty-four his eyesight was failing fast and both his hands shook constantly. So his grainy family group hadn't come out quite as he'd intended.

It was oblong in shape, five inches by four. The entire right-hand side was taken up by the back of his terraced house and a side view of old Alice, Jasmin's great aunt, who was sitting obliviously in a deck chair on the patio. The middle strip of the picture showed a rock garden which gave on to a border of orange wallflowers and then a stretch of lawn speckled with dandelion fluff. Finally, on the picture's extreme left, within a strip no more than a couple of inches wide, stood all four Piasts.

Old Frank had been so worried about fitting them all in that he'd made them squash up against one another like sardines. Only Jasmin herself appeared in full. She was wearing a gathered calf-length green skirt, a white blouse, and white high heels. She was standing in such a way that she looked pregnant. Her hair hadn't been cut so short then. Strands of it had streaked across her clouded face.

Behind her was the unobscured half of her lovely

younger sister Kate. Bobbed dark hair, a glimpse of sun-tanned face, an arm and a leg of a beige flying suit, and a single pink espadrille.

Right next to Kate, their heads almost touching, was Eileen. And Eileen was overlapped by Sidney, who was standing a couple of feet away from Jasmin. Both her parents looked desperately out of sorts, Sidney in a smart char-coal suit, Eileen in a russet woollen dress that had been too warm for the day. Old Frank had clearly asked Sidney to incline his head toward Jasmin. As a result he looked either drunk or mad. And, for good measure, old Frank had chopped off both his feet just above the ankle.

It was a very silly photo indeed. As a family unit they seemed perplexed, disoriented, horribly vulnerable, as if they were all about to be swept up in the fist of some in-visible giant. It was hard to imagine four people looking less comfortable with one another.

But Jasmin had got hold of a print because it appealed to her lively sense of the absurd. Originally she'd intended to base a comic line drawing on it, perhaps even a cartoon with a caption. In the end she'd simply pinned it to the bulletin board in her room along with all her ephemera. Her family wasn't, after all, a fit subject for levity. It never had been. The photo remained as a kind of icon at which Jasmin dutifully sacrificed her peace of mind, year in, year out.

But there was absolutely no reason why she should now be taking the photo to St. David's. No reason that was clear to Jasmin. She didn't want to carry all this extra emotional baggage around with her. She just couldn't seem to shake herself free, especially now that she saw her parents and sister so infrequently.

She knew that, as a unit, her family was dying. Dying from self-inflicted wounds, but dying none the less. As the elder child, Jasmin felt she had a responsibility to heal these wounds. And she genuinely regarded her failure to do so as a perversion, a dark, sticky, and writhing thing that cast its shadow over every other aspect of her life.

That was why she'd taken such notice of what Lacy had said to her in the pub. *So it takes something out of the ordinary to bring you all together, then?* Correct, absolutely correct. First he'd honed in on the photo, and then he'd said that to her.

Lacy. Terence Lacy. Sitting beside her and singing along to the music on her cassette.

A Welshman in shorts who ate hazelnuts for wisdom.

But she was going to St. David's with him for fun, she reminded herself. For a break.

At that stage, Terence Lacy was nothing more than a diversion.

7

THEY DIDN'T SPEAK MUCH ON THE FIRST LEG OF THE JOURNEY.
Jasmin cracked the occasional hazelnut for Lacy. He sang
along heartily with the cassette music but he also seemed
to be concentrating hard on his driving. There were plenty
of questions that Jasmin didn't feel up to asking him. Not
yet anyway.

Eventually they stopped for a snack at a motorway service station. It was a sultry day. Jasmin was beginning to
feel languid, the way she often did on long car journeys.

So who's looking after your kids this weekend? she
asked Lacy on the way up to the cafeteria.

He shot her a sideways look that could have seemed

withering on a fiercer face. Someone well qualified, he replied, and that, too, could have sounded surly if his tone had been less benign.

Jasmin felt mildly flustered. No more questions, she told herself. Later perhaps, but not now.

At once Lacy started to talk with his old gusto, mainly about Wales and its history. (Only then did it occur to Jasmin that the sheer Welshness in him seemed to have burgeoned since she'd first met him. Only a week before even his accent had been barely noticeable. Jasmin wondered idly whether he was honing a nationality merely for her benefit. But what if he was? What if he was?)

He ate prodigiously, returning to the counter several times for pastries and trifles after a huge mixed grill. Jasmin made do with a mug of coffee. She had a shock when she looked inside her purse. She'd brought only four pounds in cash, and her credit card was in her other purse, which was now on the table beside her bed. She drank her coffee with great deliberation. She wasn't the sort of girl who liked men to do the paying. She wasn't quite sure what she should do.

On the way back to the car Lacy was almost theatrically careful to avoid contact with Jasmin. It seemed important to him to keep up the formality between them. Then, as they got moving again, he glanced two or three times at Jasmin's bag. In a peculiar way she felt sure he'd guessed that the photo was inside.

So what does your sister do? he asked.

Sorry?

Your sister, Kate, wasn't it? She works, does she?

She works, said Jasmin, nodding slowly. She's a bilingual secretary. Well, more of a personal assistant now I suppose. Quite high-powered actually.

Lacy looked impressed. I expect she gets to travel a lot?

Jasmin paused before answering. As a matter of fact, she said, she's been living in Brussels for nearly five years now.

Very nice. She must like it then?

She must. Jasmin looked out of her side window. It had never been easy for her to talk about her beautiful sister— especially to men. Jasmin was the elder of the two by only eighteen months, and, although she had no grounds for thinking in this way, she had always seen Kate as a sexual rival. Time and distance had barely affected her paranoia. Many, many years before, Jasmin had convinced herself that Kate was biding her time. Patiently biding her time until Jasmin would at last settle on a man she could really love. And then Kate would make her own move, and snatch the man away.

And she's still single? asked Lacy.

Jasmin turned and looked at Lacy. (She had an impression that he had sensed exactly how jealous of Kate she was. Exactly.) That's right, she said. And I can't see Kate getting married now. She likes enjoying herself too much for that.

It was an excruciatingly silly thing to say. And when she saw the little smile at Lacy's lips, she felt as if she'd stripped a part of herself naked in front of him.

Your mum must miss her though? Lacy said. Being over there abroad?

Jasmin shrugged. What could she say?

I thought she looked like a fine woman, your mother, in that photo.

Jasmin smiled. Again, there was nothing she could say. What was there ever to say about poor Eileen? She wished they could talk about something else. She was sure that Lacy was only being polite, but this conversation was beginning to annoy her.

She met your dad after the war, did she?

Jasmin briefly closed her eyes. Yes. He came here when the camps were liberated. (She stopped, then decided to go on.) The Germans captured him in 1941. He was in one camp after another for four years. Then he came here.

My God, said Lacy, frowning. That must have left a mark on him.

Well he never talks about it. (Jasmin tried to chuckle.) Except when it comes to Germans. He loathes them, the entire German nation. Men, women, children. He thinks they're like a plague. You know, like a Biblical plague? (Now *please* shut up about it, she thought.)

Lacy nodded. He looked grim. But Sidney Piast was a grim subject. Jasmin had always regarded her father as a kind of transient. England had never meant much to him. All those years ago Sidney had left his heart in Warsaw. And Jasmin still dreaded that one day he would go back home for good—without her mother.

For Jasmin knew just how things stood between her Sidney and Eileen. They had long since stopped loving each other. That in itself wasn't a disaster. But unlike other aging couples they'd found nothing to put in love's place.

Good people, Lacy had called them all. Good people. And he'd been right. They were essentially decent, all four of them, the sort of people who might one day inherit the earth but who wouldn't make any excessive claims for themselves in the meantime. So why in God's name did they all have to tear at one another so?

Jasmin knew that her obsession with her own family was unhealthy. She knew it was morbid. But knowing didn't help. And when she'd turned to her friends, years before, in confusion and sometimes even in tears, they had responded for the most part without sympathy. That's how families are, they'd told her, shrugging, as if she were being hopelessly unrealistic to expect anything different. But Jasmin had gone on needing things to be different, to be better.

Often she prayed to God, pleading with Him not to let anything happen to her family, anything final or crushing or chaotic. Not yet, not yet. Not until she'd roused herself and made a genuine attempt at resolution, at reconciliation. And she knew that she was running out of time . . .

So what age are your parents? Lacy asked suddenly.

Jasmin started. It seemed for a moment that Lacy had actually been following her sequence of thoughts. I'm not quite sure, to be honest. They're in their late sixties though, both of them. Why?

No reason. (He smiled at her, and glanced for the last time at her bag.) Just nosey.

And then, to Jasmin's relief, he started to sing again. But she was left with the strangest feeling. It was as if Lacy had been playing with her. As if he had known in advance all these things about her family, but had just been wanting her to say them—and think them—purely for his benefit. It was as if, in some obscure way, he had been testing her.

There! he cried, soon after they'd crossed into Wales and flecks of rain began to speckle the windscreen. What did I tell you? Nowhere on earth like it for rain!

He seemed quite delighted. I'll say this though, he went on. The rain in Wales is never as *vindictive* as the rain in England.

Jasmin smiled at him. But her smile quickly faded. She saw that Lacy's eyes were ranging back and forth across the dashboard. In a flash it occurred to her that he didn't know how to operate the windscreen wipers. Luckily she'd driven an Escort once herself. She pointed out the lever on the steering column.

How long have you had this car? she asked him.

Not long enough! he replied, laughing.

Jasmin tried very hard not to think her next thought. It was no good. The idea that she was sitting in a stolen vehicle had flooded her mind.

You've hired it, have you? she said several minutes later.

What's that, love?

This car. You've hired it?

No, it's borrowed! From a friend. Just for the weekend, like.

Jasmin turned and searched his profile. Did he look like a car thief? Did he? She really had no idea. His facial features were fine. They didn't seem to belong with his sturdy physique. His eyebrows were no more than wisps, his nose small and pointed. He had full lips, and, as on that Sunday lunchtime, he seemed not to have shaved. He scratched his head through the knit hat.

I don't know the first thing about him, thought Jasmin. I don't know the first thing about him and I'm completely in his hands.

The last stage of the journey took them through some of the bleakest country that Jasmin had seen in Britain. It was years since she'd last visited Wales, and she hadn't exactly been pining for the place in the meantime. Rain was peppering the fields from a low white sky. When Lacy tuned the radio in to a cricket match, they heard that it was a marvelously sunny day back in the midlands of England.

At last they began to see signs for St. David's. Jasmin wondered how long it would be before Lacy made his move. She was under no illusions. He was bound to make it sooner or later. He wasn't that much different from the anodyne men she'd known before.

She intended to protest if he hadn't booked separate

rooms after all. But she didn't expect them. And she wasn't going to make a big public thing out of her protest. She'd accepted that in the end she would sleep with Lacy. She was a grown-up girl who had always looked after herself. Sleeping with men was just something that she did. By and large she found it preferable to sleeping on her own. Sometimes she wished that the choice of men had been a little wider. That was all.

The hotel had two stars and stood on the edge of the little town. (Lacy insisted, quite correctly, on calling it a city.) The girl at the desk greeted him with familiarity. She told him he must be frozen in his flimsy clothes. Jasmin felt left out as they laughed together, checking the reservations in the register.

Two single rooms, Lacy was saying. One for me and one for my probation officer here.

Jasmin smiled at him apologetically. (Not for the last time that weekend, she realized what dull company she herself could be.) The girl pulled two keys from the wall behind her. Jasmin glanced at the register. Lacy hadn't been lying at all. He'd genuinely booked two rooms in advance, one of them in Jasmin's name.

There you are my loved one, Lacy said as he gave her a key. All above board. Look, they're not even next door to each other. Right then, I'll meet you in the porch here in—what?—half an hour? Give you time to freshen up a bit. Then I'm going to show you the Cathedral. It looks so much better in the wet. The rain brings out the colors in the stones, you see.

Jasmin's room was in a corridor above the bar. It had a double bed even though it was a single room. There was also a walk-through bathroom, a small color television, plenty of cupboard space. There wasn't much of a view—just the roof of the hotel extension.

She flicked through the folder of literature on the dressing table. The hotel restaurant had been praised in a number of eating guides. Quickly she unpacked, made and drank a cup of tea, then went back down to wait for Lacy. She wasn't at all sure what his game was. The separate rooms had thrown her rather more than she cared to admit.

Lacy arrived late. He was wearing a pristine bottle-green oilskin over his singlet and shorts, and a sou'wester on his head. He looked as if he'd strayed in from a situation comedy.

I've booked us in for dinner here tonight, he told Jasmin with great seriousness. I hope that's agreeable to you. The food is damn good. And eating at the home base cuts out the driving, you see . . .

He opened the door and ushered Jasmin out into the car park. Then, for the best part of three hours, he showed her the sights of St. David's.

Jasmin couldn't help but be impressed—by the sights themselves, but more particularly by Lacy's knowledgeable, even learned, commentaries. Even if he'd been reading it all up in a guidebook beforehand, his memory was quite phemonenal.

First he gave her a tour of the Cathedral (which was indeed an unimagined pleasure), then the ruined Bishop's Palace, and then, when the rain had slowed off to a drizzle, the remains of a tiny Dark Age church very close to the sea. On the way they passed a pretty little wishing well, whose waters had a reputation for healing. Jasmin threw in a handful of coins and stooped to wet her fingers.

Lacy was good enough not to inquire after her ailment.

If he had asked, she wasn't at all sure what she would have told him.

They walked on into the town center. The rain had stopped, so Lacy took off his sou'wester. He looked unearthly with his shaven head, his oilskin, and his bare legs. Jasmin watched people's eyes widening as they approached. From a rack outside a gift shop he bought a pot-bellied glazed clay dragon.

There you are, he said, presenting it to Jasmin. A souvenir of a rainy day in Wales. It'll liven up that old room of yours back home.

Jasmin looked into his eyes and searched for a hint of sarcasm. There was none to be found. She took the dragon and thanked him.

It's yours, mind, he said. Don't go giving it away now.

By the time they got back to the hotel the bar was open. Lacy downed his first two pints of Bass before taking off his oilskin. He seemed to know the barman well, but he'd used the same boisterously familiar tone with the woman at the gift shop and with the other sightseers in the Cathedral. He was evidently in tremendously good humour.

Jasmin's mood was more uncertain. She knew that, at some point, she was going to have to talk to him about money. She saw no real alternative to letting him pay now, then settling up when they got back home. But she felt so feckless, so girlish, for bringing the wrong purse. It was so *unlike* her.

When Lacy decided that it was time, the two of them went to their respective rooms to change for dinner. Jasmin placed her dragon on top of the television set, stripped down to her underwear, and stood at the window. Two large black birds were waddling about in the puddles at the far end of the extension roof.

Right on the edge, Lacy had said, *Where the land meets the sea*. Another kind of limbo, thought Jasmin, neither one thing nor the other. She wished she'd brought a dress or a smart skirt. All she had was jeans and jumpers and a nightie. She'd forgotten to bring makeup too. She was very light on makeup as a rule. But this, she felt, was one of her off days, and her face could have done with some help.

She looked over her shoulder at herself in the dressing table mirror. There wasn't an ounce of spare flesh on her, but no one could have called her too thin. She had a handsome body. Only Jasmin herself refused to acknowledge it. What's going to happen next, twilight girl? she said to her reflection. How is this going to end?

But already Jasmin sensed that only Lacy could answer that.

8

IT WAS JUST AS WELL THAT LACY HAD BOOKED A TABLE. THE large L-shaped restaurant was completely packed. Lacy pulled out a chair for Jasmin. He was wearing an immaculate dinner jacket and black tie, which made him look stunningly overdressed in that company. Jasmin on the other hand felt more chastened than ever by her own knockabout sweater and mud-spattered shoes.

The meal progressed slowly and uncomfortably. During the first two courses Lacy seemed distracted. Jasmin wondered if it was the effect of the drink. (He kept ordering pints of Bass from the bar, as well as sharing a bottle of Muscadet with her.) The service was just a little intrusive,

but the food—salmon, crab, simply cooked vegetables—
was pleasing, and Jasmin didn't feel inclined to worry about
Lacy's preoccupation. It was his game. They were playing
it, presumably, by his rules.

Then while they were awaiting the sweet trolley he produced a small package from his jacket pocket. He reached
over and placed it on Jasmin's side of the table. He looked
awfully sheepish. Whatever it was, it had been gift-
wrapped, and tied neatly with a yellow bow. Jasmin felt the
blood rushing in her head. Flowers, then the dragon, now
this. What was he up to?

It's nothing but a token, he said. A birthday present.
For your mum.

My mother? Jasmin's face fluttered between ex-
pressions.

I thought she looked like a fine woman, you see, in your
picture.

Well that's very kind, said Jasmin, picking the package
up. It was cylindrical, a couple of inches high, and extremely
light. Jasmin fingered the delicate satin bow. The question
was echoing inside her head long before she asked it: How
did you know it was my mother's birthday?

It's on Wednesday, he replied playfully. Am I right or
am I right?

Yes. But how do you know that?

He smiled into his lap and adjusted his napkin. The sheep-
ishness had gone. Jasmin put down the package. She was
panicking. The look in her eyes had suddenly become quite
wild.

Please tell me, she said as levelly as she could. Don't do
this. Please tell me.

Oh, come on my love, relax! It was on that board in

your room. You know? You'd written a note to remind yourself and pinned it up. Remember?

Jasmin capitulated into a laugh. She ran her hand down the side of her face. I'm sorry, she said. I . . . I'm a bit funny about my family. I just . . . worry about them. (She picked up the package again.) But this is really very good of you. You're . . . I don't know, you're just so surprising.

It was the first personal remark that either of them had made that day. And it had a strange effect on Lacy. Momentarily he seemed to have been thrown off balance. It was as if he'd seen intimacy approaching like a runaway truck, crashing through his carefully contrived barricades of formality. He began to talk busily, about Dyfed, about the places he wanted to show her on the following day. He said something about an island off the coast.

He was talking more loudly than before, and watching the middle-aged couple at the next table, who quietly looked back.

The only trouble with this part of the world, he said, choosing some strawberries from the trolley, is the weather. I've never been here when it wasn't belting down.

Ah, well then, said the woman at the next table, leaning forward as if on cue, you've been most unfortunate. We've been coming here for six years, and this is the first bad day we've had. Isn't that right, Will?

Her husband nodded at Lacy with sparkling eyes. A conversation sprang to life between the two tables. Jasmin didn't mind. She was ready to follow Lacy's lead.

The couple turned out to be schoolteachers from Glamorgan. Lacy suggested that they should all take their coffee together in the lounge. In time the coffees gave way to brandies. And all the while Lacy continued to order pints of Bass

48

from the bar. He was well into double figures before Jasmin stopped counting.

The Welsh couple were clearly charmed by his theories on education, theories which he trotted out without any sign of previous consideration. They ended up by inviting Jasmin and Lacy to drop in on them if ever they were near Neath. By the time they withdrew, the lounge was almost empty.

Jasmin, alone again with Lacy, had drunk too much herself to know what to say or do. She sat in silence, marveling at his capacity for alcohol. Perhaps, for all his bluster, he really was sexually shy? Jasmin was quite prepared to lead him, if that was what he wanted. But she needed a definite signal from him first. The last thing she wanted to do was offend him.

So you're having a good time, are you? he asked, looking at his watch.

Yes, said Jasmin. It's lovely. It's a lovely break.

Good. Good. He was fiddling with his cuffs. Jasmin wondered if she should tell him about the money. But she just couldn't face it. Not now. In the morning. Not now.

Tired? he asked her.

I am actually. (Here we go, she thought, almost with relief. Now we're coming to the main business of the evening.)

Better get on up and turn in then, my love. I'll see you down here for breakfast. Eight-thirty. Same table.

Jasmin chewed on the inside of her lip. Lacy was simply swirling the beer around in his glass. There was no signal to be had there. None at all. She thanked him profusely for the meal. He got to his feet as she made to leave the lounge. For a moment she thought he was going to shake her hand. But again he studiously avoided all contact.

Until tomorrow, then, he said.

Until tomorrow.

When she was back in her room she left the door un-locked. Just in case. She undressed, took a quick bath, and crawled under the bedclothes. She'd switched the television on for company. The reception was so poor that she could barely make sense of the old black-and-white film that was showing.

In the greenish light shed by the picture she felt queasy, nonplussed, even guilt-stricken. She'd never before met anyone who operated like Lacy. Down in the lounge she'd considered taking the lead with him. Now she appreciated how impossible that would have been. He was leading her all the time. He was leading her when he was with her. He was even leading her when he was somewhere else. She was sharp enough to realize this after a single day in his company.

Jasmin looked at the dragon on the television set. Along-side it she'd placed his present for her mother. Just what kind of a man was this Terence Lacy? And what, she began to wonder, could he possibly want from her?

9

JASMIN COULDN'T SLEEP. THE FILM HAD FINISHED, THE TELE-vision stations had closed down, and Jasmin couldn't sleep. She switched on her bedside lamp and plumped up the pillows behind her head. Then she rummaged in her bag until she found the photo of her family.

The sight of it made her feel terribly upset. By shoving it carelessly into her bag she'd creased the top right hand corner. A stark white diagonal line now disfigured the picture, just above where old Alice was sitting. She tried to smooth out the crease with her thumb. It did no good at all. Jasmin valued neatness very highly. In her eyes the thing was completely spoiled.

She rummaged again in the bag and found her nail scissors. With immense, still rather drunken, concentration, she cut the photo right down the middle. In the left half, the four Piasts now stood centralized. In the right half there was old Alice and the crease. Jasmin tore this latter half in two and dropped it into the waste bin at the side of the bed. It didn't seem to her to be a strange thing to do. Not at that time. Not then.

She held the remaining section of the photo up to the light. The four Piasts. These were the people who mattered. Old Alice had never really belonged in the study anyway. The four mournful Piasts, waiting in a huddle for the giant's fist to scoop them up once and for all.

And then she recalled that look on Lacy's face, back in her room at home, when he'd turned away from the picture. A look of such sorrow, such discomposure, such alarm. Yes, alarm. As if he'd suddenly awoken from a harrowing dream. No, it was more complicated than that. It was as if he'd just woken up in the middle of *someone else's* nightmare, a nightmare which he'd previously believed to have been his own. Oh, God, thought Jasmin, Please stop me thinking like this. Please stop my mind from running away from me.

But immediately she began to play a bleary kind of game with herself. She imagined that Lacy had somehow gatecrashed old Frank and Alice's tea party. He was standing there, beaming, behind old Frank as he took the photo. Then the four Piasts were peeling themselves apart. Now Jasmin was introducing Lacy to the other three.

And what were Lacy's first impressions? What did he make of these three? What did he make of the three most important people in Jasmin's life? She peered at the picture and tried to put herself in Lacy's position.

Sidney's most striking characteristic was surely his foreignness. He'd been in England for over forty years but his English was still dreadfully clumsy. He had a determined handshake though, a calloused ex-engineer's hand. And under his shock of grey hair he was still good looking.

He was also extremely reserved. That would have come across at once. It was as if he'd brought his own private little Iron Curtain from the East. He gave the impression that his face was just a front, a register for options which were all equal in weight. Sidney Piast, a silent impenetrable man. A man who didn't seem to care very greatly.

And then there was Eileen. What would Lacy have made of Eileen? He'd already said that she looked nice. And she did, too, in a stiff, businesslike sort of way. Like Jasmin she'd never carried any excess weight. But she'd never been attractive. Her face had always looked too haunted to attract people. Lacy, like just about everyone else, would have seen a straightforward late-middle-aged woman. He couldn't have guessed how often Jasmin worried about her, pitied her, fought with her.

But what of Kate? The main point about Kate was her loveliness, her sheer unassuming physical loveliness. She would have shaken Lacy's hand without flirtatiousness. (Kate had never needed to learn how to flirt.) But as she drifted away, he would have chased her with his eyes. He'd have watched her as he sipped from his teacup, gone on watching her as he picked triangular sandwiches from the plates that Eileen proffered.

Kate had that effortless kind of beauty that made men go shifty and alert. Jasmin had seen it happening time after time. It had nothing to do with the clothes she wore. (Kate tended to disguise herself as a toddler, all pastel dungarees and chunky socks, sometimes even bows and clips in her hair.)

Her skeletal, wide-eyed appearance had never seemed to offend other women either. Women of all ages gravitated toward Kate, as if she possessed a secret unknown to the vast majority of womankind. And the unspoken premise of all her relationships, of all her *conversations*, was that she belonged in a bedroom. Oh, yes, Lacy would have enjoyed Kate. Lacy wouldn't have taken Kate to the Welsh coast and put her in a separate room.

Oh, damn, damn, damn, murmured Jasmin, slipping the truncated photo back into her bag. *Good people. Good people.* And what would those good, wretched people have made of Terence Lacy?

They'd have seen a youngish Welsh scaffolder with no hair. That's all. A man with children who spent his weekends fighting pretend battles and taking wry girls to the seaside. Sidney might possibly have admired his spirit. Kate and Eileen would have found him quaint. And common.

Damn, damn, she muttered again as she switched off the lamp and nestled down in the bed. Her door was still unlocked. She couldn't be bothered to get up and lock it. Before she at last dropped off to sleep she had a semidelirious vision of Lacy standing stark naked at the foot of her bed. He was pointing his penis at her like a shotgun. There were black wells of nothing where his eyes should have been.

And as Jasmin slept she dreamed. It was a dream unlike any that she had dreamed before. She was inside a palace, a deserted, high-ceilinged palace room. Beyond the walls, all around her, she could hear the sea. There was light to either side, but straight ahead it was dark, murky dark. And through the dark she could distinguish the outline of a door. Behind her, beyond her, men were singing. (It was the singing that she'd thought she'd heard in her room back at home.) The voices were urging her forward into the darkness, forward to the door. *It's happening now,* said a man's voice from nowhere. *This is it, now. Don't be frightened. It's what you've been waiting for . . .*

She woke up confused and very cold. She reached for her watch. It was only two o'clock. Immediately the first wave of song billowed up from the bar down below. Men's voices, powerfully shrill. After two or three minutes of a poignant anthem the singing ceased. Jasmin was trembling. She heard chatter and laughter, the chink of glasses, a brief silence, then another wave of sound.

For ten minutes or so this pattern repeated itself. The noise was loud enough to wake up everyone in the hotel. Jasmin slipped back into her sweater and jeans and tiptoed down the stairs. She was quite ready to find the bar empty, willing to accept that it had been an aural hallucination. But she had to find out. The voices were urging her on.

The main door was ajar. There was only one small light on, behind the bar itself at the far end of the room. A dozen men were standing in a semicircle, looking to their conductor, waiting to be cued in. The conductor was Lacy, in his shirtsleeves now, his tie unravelled and draped around his neck.

He counted one-two-three in a whisper, raised a forefinger, and the luxuriant melodies swelled up yet again. Jasmin watched closely from behind the door. Each singer seemed to be transfixed. It was as if the song were merely using them as its medium, as its way of rising up from oblivion and assuming a freshly definable form.

Jasmin couldn't guess what it was about. It just seemed to be loaded with time and truth and sadness. And she saw the look on Lacy's upturned face. Exactly the same look as she'd seen two weeks before in her own room. She saw again the shadow that lay behind his eyes and his mouth.

55

She sensed the darkness coursing through his entire body, swirling, eddying, scouring his insides clean away. And she sensed at that moment that he had the power to turn her life inside out like a cloth pocket.

She crept back up to her room hoping that he hadn't seen her. She felt sure that he hadn't wanted to be seen. Not like that. Not by her. The rain drummed hard against her window and the song soared on and on. Soon afterward she fell asleep and she didn't wake up until eight the next morning.

When she went down for her breakfast, Lacy was gone.

10

LACY WASN'T AT THE TABLE. HE WASN'T IN THE FOYER. JASMIN went to his room and knocked, and he wasn't there either. She returned to the foyer, stood at the glass doors, and watched the rain slanting across the car park. Despite what Lacy had said, it looked as vindictive as any rain Jasmin had ever seen.

The girl at the desk was sorting newspapers. Nice to have it heavy for a change, she said to Jasmin, with a completely straight face.

Jasmin craned her neck and saw that the cherry-red Escort was no longer parked outside the hotel.

She closed her eyes, then counted very slowly to twenty

before returning to her room. Methodically, hardly daring to think about the mess she was in, she packed her bag. Only at the last minute did she decide that she would take the pot-bellied dragon.

Things really didn't look too promising. She was as far inside Wales as it was possible to be. It was a Sunday. She had no transport and virtually no money. And the rain didn't look as if it was going to stop until the middle of the following week. Jasmin stepped out into the corridor.

Jasmin! I'm sorry I'm so late, my love!

It was Lacy, thundering up the stairs in his oilskin and sou'wester. His face was bloated with rain and exhaustion. I've been out fishing with some of the boys, he panted as he dashed past her. Out since the crack of dawn. God but it's a wet one! I'll see you downstairs in two shakes.

Jasmin said nothing, tried to think nothing. Whatever happened during the rest of that day, it couldn't be as disastrous as being stranded in St. David's. Could it?

Lacy washed, shaved, and came down to breakfast in his least outlandish ensemble to date. A pair of brown needlecords, a white roll-necked pullover, and Wellingtons—none of which seemed to have been worn before. (Had he raided a men's outfitter's as well as stealing the car? Jasmin was too relieved to see him to care.)

They ate a good breakfast. Afterwards Jasmin remained at the table while Lacy went upstairs to collect his things. He returned quickly, folding the receipt for the hotel bill into his wallet. Had he wanted her to see that he'd paid?

Jasmin took a deep breath. Look, she began, closing her eyes, I've been a complete idiot and left my money in my other purse, at home . . .

Lacy simply widened his eyes, then walked behind her and drew back her chair, allowing her to stand.

As soon as we get back, Jasmin persisted, I'll settle up my half of all the expenses.

You'll do no such thing, Lacy told her, grinning now, and ushering her ahead of him into the foyer.

No. I insist. Absolutely. Really I do, Jasmin said, too loudly, over her shoulder.

Is that right? Well, we'll see then, love. We'll see . . . And then Lacy put an end to it by saying his protracted farewells to the staff.

They headed southward out of St. David's. Jasmin, resentful that the money question still hadn't been resolved, saw a long and probably futile day stretching ahead of her. Why is this happening to me? she thought. Why?

Soon the sky grew a little paler, the rain became a little less insistent.

Tell me, said Jasmin before she could stop herself, This isn't a stolen car, is it?

My goodness, I should say not! cried Lacy, feigning shock.

Honestly? I mean, you would tell me if it was, wouldn't you?

Cross my heart and hope to die. My, what sort of a fellow do you take me for?

(That's a very good question, thought Jasmin.)

Can I ask you something else? she said. She'd decided to go for broke.

Go on then. As long as you don't act up if you don't like the answer.

What made you shave your hair off?

I didn't have much say in that, my love. (He smiled, then began to run his fingers over his freshly shaven cheek.) It started coming out in handfuls when I was six. Alopecia, they called it. I had this wig to begin with. Can you imagine?

A kid of six in a wig! Anyway, I've been as bald as a coot since I was eight years old.

Jasmin looked at him, wide eyed. He was rubbing his cheek harder now, almost massaging it. Oh, Lacy, she gasped, I'm so sorry. I didn't mean to be so rude. (It was the first time she'd called him by his name. And she used his surname, the name by which she'd always thought of him.)

Don't worry yourself, he said. He glanced at her and took his hand from his face. We just used to say I'd lost my Celtic fringe! And my head's been coming in and out of fashion all my life.

He put one of Jasmin's cassettes into the machine, and turned the volume up quite high. It wasn't the time or the place to ask about his kids, his wife. That would have to come later. Later.

Look, he said eventually. I think it's eased off now. We can start walking.

They parked the car near a church and headed in the direction of a misty patch of blue sky. It took more than an hour to reach the place where Lacy wanted to be. Sometimes he led the way off the coastal path, taking them across fields and walls and sodden undergrowth that reached as high as Jasmin's waist.

Rain and fog hovered close by all the time. It wasn't really a day to be out walking. Once or twice they crossed paths with other intrepid ramblers, men and women who approached with uncertain smiles but were glad to respond to Lacy's breezy conversation.

The landscape looked more hospitable than on the previous day. Jasmin thought it was a still, docile land. She mentioned this to Lacy.

Oh, you'd be surprised! he laughed back. You'd be surprised, my love. And he launched into a diatribe about the landforms of Dyfed, the Preseli mountains, and about an ancient Welsh tale in which this part of the country had been magically denuded of its people, its farms, and its animals.

Jasmin listened patiently enough. But she couldn't shake off her baser suspicions about Lacy. Every now and then she wondered whether he was going to want to make love in some bracing open place. He did look as if he might be the sort. Yet he continued to respect her body space, and on several stretches of the terrain they had to walk in single file.

Suddenly, at a spot of no apparent significance, Lacy stopped in his tracks and pointed out to sea. This is as close as we'll get, he said, The Island . . .

Jasmin came up alongside Lacy and narrowed her eyes. She thought that she could make out a shape through the sea mist but she couldn't be at all sure. She was about to ask Lacy what they were seeing, but then she saw the change in him.

He was standing at attention. The shadow was there again behind his eyes. She could sense the darkness again, the darkness that had taken possession of him.

He began to declaim in a language which was unintelligible to her—presumably Welsh. As with the singing of the previous night, Jasmin had no inkling of what it meant. But again it sounded old, sad, talismanically true. The words seemed to form a kind of invocation, spilling from Lacy's black mouth almost of their own accord.

Soon he fell silent. He looked badly buffeted.

Well, what was all that about? asked Jasmin, a little frightened and a little bored. The wind around them was cold and squally. There wasn't another living soul in sight, and, to be quite honest, she couldn't see anything that remotely resembled an island.

The Tale of Branwen, he replied at once. It's a story that goes with this land . . . Long, long ago there was a party of seven men, the only survivors of a ruinous war. They were carrying the talking head of Bran, their giant king. Bran had told them that they would come to Gwales in Penfro—that island, out there. For as long as they liked they would be able to feast in a palace on the island, and they would know no sorrow. But Bran gave them a single instruction. It was this . . .

Jasmin looked at her feet. She was beginning to feel embarrassed. Why was he telling her this fairy tale? Why had he brought her to this godforsaken place? Why had she *let* him bring her?

In the palace there would be three doors, Lacy went on. Two would be open. The third would be closed. On no account were they to open that third door . . .

Lacy paused. The effort of telling the story seemed to be taxing him. But Jasmin had forgotten her embarrassment. She was looking at him now with interest. The palace by the sea. The closed door. She didn't want to sound like Eileen, but this was just what she'd been *dreaming* about.

Yes? she said. So what happened?

Lacy drew himself up. The shadow had left him. He looked startlingly boyish. Boyish and apprehensive.

The seven men found the palace. They went inside, and at once all their memories of grief and suffering slipped from them. For eighty years they enjoyed the most perfect happiness. The years passed like so many minutes. No one grew older. No one wanted for anything. But then they began to wonder what lay behind the closed door. And at last one of the men could restrain himself no longer. He went to the door and he opened it, and out they all looked, at the sea and at the land far beyond.

Lacy cleared his throat. As those men looked, he went

on, They remembered every evil that they had ever suffered. They remembered all the friends and family they had ever lost. All the miseries of their past lives came flooding back to them. And it was so sudden, so crushing, *it was as if all the bad in their lives was happening to them there, for the first time, on that very spot on which they were standing* . . .

For some moments the two of them stood side by side in silence. The island—if the shape had indeed been an island—was completely obscured now by the mist. It was possible to believe that it had never been there at all. Jasmin turned away. Look, she said unsteadily, I think I dreamed about all that last night. The palace and the door. I dreamed about them.

Lacy laughed. Well I should imagine you'll probably dream about them again now! he said.

I'm being serious. You don't believe me, do you? (The color had left Jasmin's cheeks.) I really did dream about them! Only it was me who was inside the palace. And there was singing, in the distance. The singing was making me move toward the door . . .

She looked up at Lacy. And when I woke up, she continued, I heard you and your friends, down in the bar.

What's that, love? He looked puzzled.

You and your friends. Singing. I came down and I saw you.

Lacy knitted his brows. I wasn't in the bar last night, he said with a smile. I turned in just after you. I had to be up early, you see. The fishing.

I *saw* you! cried Jasmin.

You saw something, Lacy replied, shrugging. But it wasn't me. And there weren't any singers in the bar last night. We can ring the hotel and check, if that would put your mind at rest. Come on now, I'm starving. And I've got a hamper from the hotel in the trunk of the car.

11

THEY HAD THEIR PICNIC STANDING BESIDE THE OPEN CAR trunk. Fish mousses, game pie, a selection of cheeses, perfect little crème brûlées. Lacy opened a liter bottle of French table wine and they drank most of it between them.

By now the sun had broken through, but Jasmin's jeans and shoes were absolutely soaked. An English couple with three children had parked nearby for their own lunch. Lacy invited them to share the last of the food and wine, then played an uproarious game of tag with the children.

He's pretty good with kids, isn't he? said the English father to Jasmin.

Jasmin nodded. She was tired out, dizzy with the wine,

thoroughly unsettled by the business of the palace and the door and the male voice choir. Why should Lacy have lied to her about the singing? What good did it do him? It wasn't anything to be ashamed of. *Had* it perhaps been a hallucination after all? But then there was the dream . . . What about the dream?

Lacy waved at her as he scudded about on the loose stones of the parking lot. She knew virtually nothing about him. And the things that she did know didn't put her at her ease. She'd known plenty of unpredictable men. She'd known a fair few liars, too. But Lacy was quite different again. He seemed to have no essential core to him. He was like a random accumulation of personalities. Now you saw one, now you saw another. Even his physical appearance seemed to be indefinable. Depending on the circumstances he could look angular or fluid, full-featured or taut-faced, downright witless or intimidatingly shrewd. He talked almost incessantly yet he gave nothing away about himself. Jasmin had never known a man who said "I" less than Lacy.

The English family got themselves together and drove off. Lacy sat next to Jasmin in the car but didn't turn on the engine. He was looking out curiously at the small cemetery that stretched between there and the church. Jasmin should have been prepared for more surprises. But she was floored by what Lacy said to her next. To be fair, Lacy himself sounded mystified, as if he'd just discovered someone else's thought inside his head.

We've lost the knack of dealing with death, he said. We belittle the dead. Oh, we give them funerals and we bury them. We do that right enough. But we've taken away the *fun* from dying, from moving on.

Jasmin shrugged. This wasn't a conversational line that she felt like pursuing. Why on earth did a scaffolder talk that way? He's making a fool of me, she thought. He's winding me up.

Lacy roused himself and turned the key in the ignition. He had to back up a little way. He twisted around and rested his arm along the top of the passenger seat.

It doesn't do to worry about dying, he said with a grin. (His face was very close to Jasmin's, kissably close. She could smell his sweat.) Everyone dies for a reason. Death is a means to an end, that's all.

Right then, said Jasmin, tilting back her head. I shall remember that.

Lacy finished backing up, then sat square in his seat again. It really is a good thing to remember, my love. You might go getting things out of proportion otherwise. I mean, how old is that great-aunt of yours? The one in the picture?

Alice? I don't know. Eighty-eight, eighty-nine.

Well, there you are then. Death is a means to an end . . . Sometimes the end isn't immediately clear.

He pulled out on to the road and they drove away from the church, from the cemetery, from the island that Jasmin hadn't seen, and from Lacy's morbid preoccupations.

Jasmin said nothing. She'd had just about as much as she could take of Lacy. She wasn't a person who stood on ceremony. But what he'd said about old Alice had been unforgivably tasteless. All she wanted now was to get back home in one piece. It had been a mistake to come with him. She should have stayed in her room and bored herself instead. Soon after they returned to the faster roads Jasmin fell asleep.

She slept soundly and awoke to find them motoring through the affluent English midlands in the midst of an early evening hailstorm. Beyond the hail, beautiful steep billows of cloud were floating stark against an azure sky.

It was display weather. A children's book composite illustration of rain, mist, cloud, and sun.

There must be a rainbow, said Jasmin, swivelling in her seat.

No, Lacy told her flatly. It was as if he were forbidding one to appear.

He began to talk. Sport, sporting records, surprising statistics. Jasmin listened, nodding politely. She just wanted to get home. She didn't mind what she had to put up with on the way. She cracked him a few more hazelnuts. Every time she caught sight of a police car she still prayed that Lacy hadn't stolen the Escort.

They stopped at a country pub and took their drinks outside into the sunshine.

Thank you very much for everything this weekend, Jasmin began, opening her bag and taking out her purse. It's been . . . an education. Can I, could I write you a check?

Pah! said Lacy with a dismissive wave, ladies don't pay.

Ladies do pay, Jasmin corrected him. That's what makes them ladies. If you won't take a check, I've got money in my other purse. We'll settle up when we get back. Please.

Lacy beamed at her. He was perched on the car-park fence. The low sun was making his bald pate twinkle, making his whole head look quite radiant. Tell me, he said then, Why don't you live in a place of your own? You must be paying out a fortune in rent for that room of yours.

Jasmin put away her purse and ran her forefinger around the rim of her glass. I find it convenient, she said slowly. It's nice to have other people around.

Ah, he said. I don't suppose you get to meet many people in your line of work?

Not many, no.

So what do you do about boyfriends?

Jasmin stared at the fence right next to where Lacy was

sitting. I can't help thinking, she said, That you're just taking the rise out of me.

She expected him to remonstrate but he didn't, so she went on.

I mean, I don't want you to get me wrong. But why exactly did you take me with you this weekend? It was very nice and everything. But why me?

He finished his beer and dangled the empty mug by its handle between his legs. You're an interesting girl, he said at length. You interest me. Oh, my princess, don't look so down in the mouth! There's nothing more to it than that. Should there be?

I don't know, said Jasmin, looking away in some confusion. You're not much like anyone I've known before.

All the better, then! he laughed. Come on. Let's make tracks.

And Jasmin accompanied him sheepishly back to the car. She was still quite unable to think straight when she was with him. It was something about his eyes. They seemed to see right inside her head. She could sense them playing havoc with the ideas that she was struggling to put into words.

Lacy pulled up outside Jasmin's house as the light was beginning to fail. She invited him in, to have a cup of tea and to sort out the money. He followed her into the kitchen and sat down.

I must thank you for my mother's present again, said Jasmin.

Lacy smiled back.

I don't know when I'll be able to give it to her, though. We don't meet up very often.

Oh, you never know, said Lacy. It could be sooner than you think. (He had that look on his face again. The look he'd had when he'd said, *So it takes something out of the or-*

dinary to bring you all together, then? A smug look. Infuriatingly smug.)

While Jasmin was filling the kettle, one of the boys came in from the living room. He looked pleased to see Lacy.

Oh, Jasmin, he said, Your mother's been on the phone. She wants you to call her back. I told her you were in Wales.

Thanks, said Jasmin, I'll do it later.

The boy drummed his fingers on the tabletop. Well actually, he went on, she said she wanted to speak to you as soon as you got back.

Jasmin sighed. She made the tea, excused herself, and took her mug upstairs, leaving Lacy to chat with the boy. It was stuffy in her room, so she opened the window. The little girl in the next garden heard the grating noise. She looked up automatically. Her eyes met Jasmin's, and at once she fled back inside her house.

She dialed Eileen's number. The phone rang for a long time at the other end. While she waited, Jasmin unfastened her bag, took out the truncated family photo and pinned it on to the bulletin board again. It was the only recent picture of her family that she had. The only record.

Sidney answered. Something had to be wrong. Sidney only ever answered the phone in emergencies.

Jasmin, he said in his uncertain English drawl, where have you been? Eileen has been trying to contact you. No, she is not here now. She is with old Frank . . .

It took no longer than it needed to, but Sidney managed to pass on the information. Old Alice had been taken seriously ill on Saturday morning. Nobody seemed to know exactly what the trouble was, but they'd got her into hospital almost immediately. Then she'd gone downhill fast.

She had died during the small hours of Sunday morning. If Jasmin had been at home to receive Eileen's calls, she could have made it to the hospital before the end.

She put down the receiver and stared out of the window. The little girl next door had reemerged. Her mother was outside, too, sitting on a stool while the girl meticulously loaded garden stones into her lap. Jasmin dialed old Frank's number. Eileen answered.

Jasmin could tell from Eileen's voice that she'd recently been crying. She gave Jasmin all the details in a kind of whisper, presumably so that old Frank wouldn't hear. Jasmin slumped against the window frame as she listened. Alice had been Eileen's only blood relative apart from Jasmin and Kate. They'd read the horoscopes in the local paper to each other for more than twenty years.

Jasmin's eyes began to water. The funeral was going to be on that Wednesday at noon. One of old Frank's nephews was doing the organizing. By a brutal coincidence Wednesday happened to be Eileen's birthday, too.

It was that dream I had, you see, she said to Jasmin. I knew something was going to happen to one of us. I just thank God it wasn't you or Kate.

Jasmin could say nothing. In the light of her own experiences with Lacy that weekend she hardly dared to think, let alone speak.

Eileen reminded her how to get to old Frank's house, for the funeral. Then she rang off.

Jasmin immediately picked up her purse from the occasional table and took it downstairs, blinking back her tears.

Lacy was no longer in the kitchen. The nothingness where he should have been was almost tangible.

He said he had to be getting home, the boy told her.

Nothing else? Jasmin's voice sounded dull, cracked.

He didn't say anything else, no.

She had neither his address nor his telephone number. He'd made a completely clean break. Or so Jasmin thought.

12

IT WAS A NARROW LITTLE STREET ON A SLOPE. JASMIN MADE sure her handbrake was on tight. There were big spots of rain on the pavement. Jasmin took her umbrella from the trunk. In her bag was Lacy's present for her mother. She really didn't know how much to tell Eileen about Lacy. She'd even considered not giving her the present at all.

None of the other cars in the street looked familiar. Eileen and Sidney hadn't yet arrived. They might have been held up waiting for Kate. Kate was going to make "every effort" to fly back from Belgium for the day. She'd probably arrive with her latest man. The latest in a line of well-heeled lovers.

Jasmin smoothed her black cotton skirt and straightened the cuffs of her jacket. She was wearing lipstick, eye shadow, a couple of dabs of blush, and she knew she was looking good. She always looked good in formal dress. But she felt guilty too, as if she were brandishing her sexuality at a grossly inappropriate time.

It won't be much different from this when Sidney or Eileen dies, she thought numbly, A handful of people taking time off work in the middle of the week, someone doing the organizing, someone making sandwiches.

Old Frank's house, terraced and tiny, looked like a scale model. He'd lived there with Alice for forty-seven years. Just the two of them. They'd never had children of their own, just Jasmin and Kate, and a few boys on old Frank's side. The curtains hadn't been closed. The front door was ajar. The walls of the hallway were streaked with damp. Floral tributes had been arranged in the front room. In the middle room old Frank was sitting in his corner chair by the window. A big slow man of eighty-six with a fizz of white hair.

Jasmin stooped to kiss him. His red face puckered, his shoulders heaved. Jasmin swallowed hard. I'm so sorry, she said. I'm so, so sorry.

He nodded and re-formed his face, the tears snaking down his cheeks.

This filthy weather, he said in his quick, clipped way. Not much of a summer is it? Not much of a July?

Old Frank's sister, a mannish woman of eighty, came in from the kitchen with a plate of cakes. She smiled at Jasmin, and told her there was some tea in the pot.

By ten-to-twelve there were nine people in the house. Eileen and Sidney arrived last of all. They looked worn out, as if the short trip across town had shattered them. Sidney nodded to Jasmin from across the room. Eileen touched her elbow, told her she looked well and thanked her for the birthday card she'd sent.

Jasmin looked down the hallway to see if Kate was on her way in. She wasn't. She hadn't made it. Her most strenuous efforts had obviously not been successful. At that moment, Jasmin felt something very close to loathing for her sister. Her selfish, busy, beautiful sister.

The hearse had arrived outside the house. So had the first following car. But Jasmin, her parents and a neighbor had to wait on the pavement for the second following car, which had been held up at a previous funeral.

It was that dream I had, you see, Eileen said again as she came under Jasmin's umbrella. I'm not often wrong. There's some greater power guiding us all along, making everything happen.

Yes, said Jasmin, and she thought of Lacy sitting in that car outside the cemetery in Wales. And she wanted to tell Eileen all about her own dream, about the singing, about what Lacy had said. But she knew that she couldn't. Not yet. Not there. Not when Eileen needed quietness and compassion.

The service was short. It was no better or worse than Jasmin had been expecting. Old Frank and Alice had been married in the same squat little church sixty-one years before. These are my people, thought Jasmin as she stared at the bowed heads in front of her. This is where I come from and I'll never really get away. Never.

When they came out of the church the weather had lifted. Just as they came to the lich gate, old Frank stopped walking. All those behind him had to stop too. He turned (awkwardly, since his sister and nephew were supporting him by his arms). Jasmin saw his twitching face, his glazed eyes. He looked back up at the church tower and he lifted his hand, ungainly, as if to protect himself from a wasp. For several moments he stood with his hand raised in his own salute, then allowed himself to be led to the car, and on to the cemetery.

It was a spillover cemetery next to a main road. Jasmin ended up standing opposite her parents. She watched them closely through the prayers and incantations. They looked so dreadfully flimsy with the cars whining past behind them. Eileen knew that Jasmin was looking. She smiled back, but that just made her seem even flimsier.

O Christ Almighty, Jasmin prayed fervently inside her head, Don't take Sidney and Eileen away from me. Please don't. Not soon. Not until . . . Not until what, though? Nothing was going to change between them all now. Deep inside her Jasmin knew that. This was how it had come to be. This was as far as the Piast family went—no further than here.

The wooden planks at the graveside were dangerously unstable. The mourners had to stand on tiptoe and look at old Alice's expensive coffin from the grass verge. The floral tributes had been arranged in a line next to the path. Jasmin fell into step with Eileen on the short walk back to the limousine.

Ah, well, said Eileen, I won't have anyone to read the stars with now . . . And it was only then that she allowed herself to cry, with her hand resting lightly on her daughter's arm.

Back at the house the numbers seemed to have swollen. There was a good deal of sideways shuffling in and out of rooms. Jasmin sat on a stool in the corner of the middle room. She ate her sausage rolls and drank her tea, aware

that one of the younger men couldn't take his eyes off her
legs.

Through the window she could see Sidney standing on
the back door step smoking a cigarette. He had his charcoal
suit on. The one he'd been wearing in old Frank's silly
photo. Jasmin knew that none of this meant anything to
him. This English family had nothing to do with him. She
could almost see the man deep inside him withdrawing
completely, pulling away from them all.

It made her scared. Sidney's sheer lack of commitment
had always frightened the life out of her. Now that he was
retired there was even less to keep him in England. And
what would happen if he decided to go back to Poland?
Jasmin knew the answer. She'd have to look after Eileen
herself. No one else would. She'd have to move back in
with her mother and then they'd tear at each other and tear
at each other until there was nothing left of either of them.

Eileen was talking with several of the others about Alice's last illness. Old Frank looked eagerly from one speaker
to another, his face all puffed up and damp. There hadn't
been much talk about Alice's life. *We've lost the knack of
dealing with death,* Lacy had said. Had he seen all this in
advance? Had he in some unfathomable way *known*?

Sidney closed the back door and came into the middle
room. He caught the eyes of both Jasmin and Eileen si-
multaneously. He jerked his head, just once, toward the
front door. Jasmin looked away, pretending that she hadn't
seen. But Eileen was already on her feet, saying that they
had to be going.

Jasmin stared at her, half in pity, half in contempt. Sidney had always called the tune. Jasmin had argued with him
so often on Eileen's behalf. So often and so bitterly. But

now she stood as well, because Sidney's signal had effectively broken up the wake.

The three Piasts paid their respects once more to old Frank, and then they were the first out of the door.

Jasmin walked up the street behind her parents. The sunshine was thin, commiseratory. Sidney had parked his car behind Jasmin's.

Why did you make us come away then? Jasmin asked him in a quiet voice loaded with rancor.

What d'you say? he asked back, turning.

Why did we have to go just then? So soon?

Carefully he lit a cigarette, and looked from Jasmin to Eileen. He was looking puzzled but Jasmin knew that it was just a pretense.

We'd stayed long enough, Jas, Eileen said quickly. It's all right. I'll be popping in to see how old Frank goes on. He's got a nurse coming in, too . . .

You didn't have to come with us anyway, said Sidney. He wasn't looking at Jasmin. He exhaled a jet of cigarette smoke over the roof of his car. You can look after yourself, no? That is what you always say—"I can look after myself." No?

Jasmin narrowed her eyes at him. But before she could say anything Eileen stepped forward. Jasmin glanced at her and immediately read the expression on her face. It said: For the love of God don't start a fight here. Not in this street, not under this sky, not today . . .

And Jasmin looked back at Sidney. A survivor of the camps. A man who knew all about pain and suffering and man's inhumanity to man. She watched him getting into the car. He's not here at all, she thought. He's no longer with us at all. In his mind, he's already gone.

So what happened to Kate, then? Jasmin asked her

mother, her voice laden with sarcasm. She got tied up, did she? Something unavoidable at the last minute?

Eileen sighed wearily. Don't start on that, Jasmin. Please. It's just not worth it.

But she should have been here. She should have been. She's got no . . . I don't know. She's got no sense of family.

Who are you to talk! Eileen said fiercely. You haven't been home since God knows when. You haven't said a civil word to your father in years. Family! She glared at the pavement in the brief silence that followed, then went on more calmly, I don't know what's happening with Kate. She rang last night and told us she couldn't come. She said she's got some news but she's going to put it in writing. I don't know with you lot. I just don't know if I'm on foot or horseback half the time.

Jasmin, red in the face now, opened her bag. I've got something for you, she said. A birthday present.

Eileen looked startled. The Piasts had stopped giving one another presents some ten years before. (At around the same time, in something like the same spirit, the girls had begun to call their parents by their Christian names.) Jasmin handed over the little gift-wrapped package. It's not from me, she said. It's from Lacy.

Lacy? said Eileen. The one with no hair?

That's right. (Jasmin was glad that she hadn't said "The one with the children?")

Eileen unwrapped it on the spot, remarking on the prettiness of the yellow ribbon. She was smiling, warily delighted.

She found a transparent plastic container, shaped like a miniature biscuit barrel. She removed the plastic lid and tipped out a tiny sandalwood carving. It was no more than a couple of inches high.

It's me! Eileen squealed. Goodness gracious it's me!

And it *was* her. Just as she'd appeared in old Frank's photo. At least, the parts of her that hadn't been obscured by Sidney. It had been exquisitely made. The drawn expression on her face, the texture of the woollen dress. You could almost sense the heat of the day, the discomfort, in the way she was standing. But in front of her there was no figure of Sidney. No figure at all. Instead there was what looked like a sprouting hazel bush.

What a marvelous funny little thing. It's so lovely! said Eileen. It's just how I looked in that picture. The one at the tea party. Did you give him the picture to copy?

No, said Jasmin. No I didn't. (She guessed at once that Lacy really had been to her room on the evening that she'd been out. He'd been to her room and he'd taken a photo of the photo.) Can I see it please?

She took the carving and revolved it in her hands. It was an amazing piece of craftsmanship. If he hadn't in fact taken a photo of his own, the man's memory for detail was supernatural. But it was far more than a simple copy. For by placing the bush—instead of Sidney's body—in front of Eileen, he'd made her look like a little girl peering out from a hiding place. Her drawn expression thus became much less mournful. It was now the expression of a child, a child immersed in a game. The anxiety was still there. But it wasn't serious anxiety. It was an anxiety that would dissolve, very soon, into excited laughter.

Eileen took the carving back. She couldn't stop grinning.

Oh, this has cheered me up no end, she said. You must give me this Lacy's address. I'll write and thank him as soon as I get home.

I've got no idea where he lives, Jasmin told her. I don't

really know the first thing about him. And I wouldn't be at all surprised if I never set eyes on him again. The last time I saw him, he left without saying goodbye. I think he just got bored with me.

Oh, go on with you, said Eileen. But I would like to thank him. I've never had anything like this before. It's so beautiful!

Jasmin watched Eileen studying the carving. It was a little piece of wood. That was all. Something that had already brought her mother a great deal of happiness. But she wished that she'd taken a look at it herself before handing it over. There was something about it that wasn't quite, well, that wasn't quite . . . healthy.

There had been something quite definitely unhealthy about Lacy himself. (All that talk about death being a means to an end . . .) But this carving was something else again. It was such a strange thing to make, for someone he'd never even met. It looked as if it had some ritual connotation, like one of those effigies that witches were supposed to stick needles into. But she couldn't take it away from Eileen now. It was too late for that.

Sidney sounded his horn. He was keen to get going. Eileen said goodbye and climbed into the car. Jasmin looked down and smiled at her father's profile. She smiled because he probably didn't mean to be so ungracious. Time had made him like that. Time and displacement and the echo of unspeakable hardships.

But she smiled at him too because he wasn't in Lacy's carving. The most stunning thing by far about that carving—featuring as it did so much that was familiar—was the fact that Sidney wasn't in it.

79

13

JASMIN KNEW THAT IT WAS BEST TO STOP THINKING ABOUT Lacy.

She'd meant what she'd said to Eileen—she didn't expect to set eyes on him again. But she had her pride, not to mention her curiosity. It irked her that Lacy had taken such pains with her at first, then simply dropped her. She felt sure that she hadn't come up to scratch in some way, and she didn't find it easy to cope with rejection.

She tried to inject a bit of dash into her sabbatical season. But now that the school holidays had started it was hard to organize anything very exciting with her friends. The weather became unpredictable, too. Jasmin spent hour after hour sitting at her window, drinking wine or coffee, listening to old records.

Lawrence, her agent, sent her a parcel which she didn't even open. She knew what was in it. The typescript of the mythological story that he wanted her to illustrate. She just wasn't ready to start working again. Not yet. She'd been looking forward to this break for too long. So she toured the travel agents instead, collecting brochures, and she set about planning a holiday.

Then the incident at the swimming pool spoiled all her enthusiasm for going away.

Normally she swam in the river, with one or two friends. But late one rainy afternoon she drove out to the indoor pool, alone. The big, booming glasshouse immediately made her feel faintly hysterical. The swarms of children made it impossible to complete a single length. Eventually Jasmin just sat on the side, dangling her feet and calves in the water.

While she was moping like this, she caught sight of Lacy.

It was nothing more than a glimpse. A view from behind as he shepherded two small boys through the footbath and into the men's changing room. Jasmin jumped to her feet and made for the women's showers. In less than five minutes she'd pulled on her clothes and was waiting at the entrance to the pool.

Her T-shirt clung to her damp back. She'd had no time to do anything with her hair. Every time the door to the men's changing room opened, her heart went high and she felt as if her head were swelling.

For nearly twenty minutes she waited. Then she went to the ticket booth and asked if there was another exit. There was none. She paid to go and sit in the observation gallery.

But as far as she could tell from there, Lacy and the children hadn't returned to the water.

By the time she reached home, she'd virtually convinced herself that the sighting had been a mirage. First the male voice choir in St. David's, now this. And her heart was still thumping, her head was still reeling. She sat in the kitchen drinking tea. I shouldn't be letting this happen to me, she thought. I haven't got enough to occupy my mind.

But the incident had made one thing absolutely clear to her. She did want to see Lacy again. There was no point in trying to deceive herself. She wasn't at all sure why it was, but she really did want to see him again. So she gathered up the telephone directory and the Yellow Pages, took them to her room, and tried to track him down.

She wasn't sure how he spelled his name. There were forty-three *Laceys,* twelve *Lacys,* and a single *Lacie* in the directory. Painstakingly she transcribed every name, address, and telephone number on to a sheet of drawing paper. The initial "T" figured in only seven of them, but she knew other men who went under christian names that weren't technically their own.

Some of the addresses looked thoroughly unlikely for a scaffolder. She put crosses against these. Then she turned to *Scaffolding Erectors* in the Yellow Pages, where she found thirty-six entries, followed by a further twenty-six under *Scaffolding Hire.* Again she copied them all out.

Finally she took the sheet to the window and stared at it for several minutes. She was hoping that one of the numbers would somehow call out to her from the paper. But as her eyes ranged back and forth across her scribbles, nothing came through. She looked at the pot-bellied dragon, which she'd placed on top of her music center, and laughed. I'm going off my head, she said to it, and laughed again.

She poured herself a glass of wine and rang three of the larger scaffolding firms, ones which had placed big advertisements. It was nearing six-thirty. She wasn't expecting much of a response.

No one answered at the first two numbers. A woman answered at the third. She was giggling.

I'm sorry to trouble you, said Jasmin, But do you have a Terence Lacy working for you?

No idea, love, said the woman, I only clean the offices. The person you need to speak to isn't here. Ring back in the morning?

Yes, thank you, yes, said Jasmin before replacing the receiver. Then she shook her head in dismay and said aloud, No, surely I can't be doing this? *Surely?*

In the days that followed she lost interest in taking a holiday. She was fed up with going abroad on her own anyway. It was six years since she'd had a proper holiday with somebody else, possibly seven.

The rain was almost incessant now. Sitting at her window night after night, Jasmin toyed with the idea of taking a look at Lawrence's typescript. But she didn't get around to opening the jiffy bag. It was the principle of the thing. She'd told Lawrence that she needed a break from work. And a break she was going to have. Even if in truth she *was* only festering, as Lacy had so cruelly put it.

But one evening she dressed herself up and walked to the pub where Lacy had introduced her to his crowd. There was a chance that he might be there.

There was more of a chance that one of the others would be there. All she needed was an address, a telephone number.

The saloon was reasonably full. She recognized the squat young man at once. The one who'd asked her if she had a job. He was sitting by a window, wearing overalls, talking busily with a much older man. Jasmin bought a glass of white wine and stood at the bar, watching him. She couldn't pretend that she liked the look of him. He was presumably a garage mechanic of some sort. His hands and temples were smeared with black grease. I'm here trying to find a man, she thought with self disgust. I'm looking for a man who doesn't want to know me.

The young man rose from his table and shook hands with his partner. Jasmin suddenly turned her back on him and gripped the edge of the bar, praying that he hadn't seen her.

She waited several minutes, then she left by a different exit. And when she got home she felt horribly low, as if she'd betrayed an important part of herself for no particularly good reason.

What she needed, she knew, was someone to talk to. Someone to express her anxieties to, about her family, about Lacy, about everything. But there just wasn't anyone. Or rather, there were plenty of people who would have listened to her; but there was no one that Jasmin felt happy to confide in.

She had a reputation, among her friends, for taking most things in her stride. That suited Jasmin. She didn't want to preserve her reputation on false grounds now. But she just didn't feel like challenging other people's perception of her. She really *needed* other people to see her in sharp, simple terms, partly because she was so confused about herself.

So this left her with no one to turn to. No one, that was, until Roland King came into the picture, as the result of a rather despicable subterfuge.

14

JASMIN TOOK TO SLEEPING LATE. ONE MORNING SHE WAS awoken by the phone at half-past eleven.

Hi, said the caller. It's your favorite man!

Jasmin was too dazed to recognize the voice immediately. It was Lawrence, her agent.

Oh, hello, she said. I'd really appreciate it if you didn't start badgering me again.

Badgering you! No, no my dear, this is a social call . . .

Lawrence was a bachelor of fifty-five. Jasmin liked him very much indeed as an agent. But she found him rather hard going when he was in this impish sort of mood. He kept the conversation light and general. He didn't even mention Jasmin's sabbatical season and what he thought of it. Eventually he got to the point and asked her out for a quiet drink, at six that evening.

Jasmin said yes mainly to get him off the line. But she had no real reason to turn him down. She didn't have anything healthier to do with her time.

When she arrived at the wine bar Lawrence stood and saluted her from a corner table. He was with two other men. Both of them stood as Jasmin approached. *A quiet drink!* Lawrence had tricked her into coming to a meeting. But it was too late to turn and leave. She'd already met their eyes and confusedly acknowledged their smiles.

Lawrence had no shame about introducing the men. One was an editor from a small local house that published material on astrology, psychology, alternative medicine, folklore. Jasmin knew him. She'd designed and illustrated some book covers for him a couple of years back.

The other man was a writer called Roland King, the author of the mythological story that Jasmin was refusing to read. He was tall, athletically built, and good-looking after a downbeat, rather embarrassed fashion. Jasmin ordered a large glass of wine, then sat back and listened.

The aim of the meeting was to persuade Jasmin to take on the job of illustrating the story. The editor did most of the talking. His firm had apparently launched a series of short books in which modern authors retold stories from British mythology. He talked about the story in question as if Jasmin had already read it. He praised Roland King for expanding on the original text, from a source called the *Mabinogion,* while staying close to its spirit. To give him his due, he sounded genuinely enthusiastic.

I didn't know, said Jasmin, when the time came to order some food, I really didn't know that there was any such thing as *British* mythology. Well, apart from King Arthur perhaps.

Oh, there is, there is! said the editor. This is an ancient land. Its stories go way back, but most people just don't know about them. They think gods and heroes means Greece and Rome.

Jasmin nodded.

I suppose, he went on, that when we say British we really mean Welsh. Celtic Welsh. The stories are quite stunning. Complex, subtle. And of course they're much more than just stories. We're dealing with belief here, our old island faith. There's a kind of magisterial truth about these texts. They . . .

Roland King began to cough. Jasmin caught his eye and he smiled at her.

Roland thinks I get carried away, said the editor, blushing rather winningly.

No, no, said Roland, still smiling at Jasmin. No, no . . .

The talking went on as they ate their meal.

When they got round to discussing fees, Jasmin realized why the editor was so keen to give her the work. It was because he was offering a pittance. He'd probably approached a whole string of prouder artists before her. But she wasn't badly offended. She didn't have a good enough track record to be able to hold out for the big money.

I'll think about it, she promised in the end. I'm sorry but I can't say anything more. I'm in the middle of a sabbatical season.

The editor and Lawrence then left rather abruptly. Jasmin still had a lot of wine in her glass. So she stayed on, facing Roland King, who began to laugh again.

Jasmin shrugged at him. He was rolling himself a cigarette.

I've seen you before, he said.

Oh, really? Where?

At a party. We were introduced. Just in passing, you know.

Jasmin smiled. She didn't remember him even though she was good at faces, and his features were attractive enough. Perhaps, she thought, the trim little beard had rendered him forgettable. Instinctively she'd always mistrusted men with beards.

I know you didn't want to be here tonight, he said. You should have turned around and left.

Jasmin didn't quite know what to say. The authors she'd met before had usually been a bit boorish about anything to do with their work.

Look, he said, I'm not a wine-bar man. Would you come to a pub with me? And have a proper drink?

Jasmin looked at him, surprised. He clearly lacked confidence. Up to that point he'd hardly spoken to her. And whenever he had, he'd peeled off his wire rims and buffed them methodically. Jasmin had presumed, up to that point, that he'd found her rather brash and unlikeable. Quiet men sometimes did.

I don't mind, she said. There was nothing for her back at home. Nothing.

They set off towards a fashionable city-center pub, a crowded single room near the playhouse. Jasmin was intrigued by the way Roland walked. He was a big man, a couple of inches over six feet, but his body seemed to sag from the shoulders, and he moved with long, slightly flat-footed strides. Jasmin kept snatching sidelong glances at him. It was as if he was being worked by a puppeteer who'd let some of the tension go out of his strings.

So what made you write the story? Jasmin asked after he'd fetched a couple of beers.

Oh, vanity, he replied. There's never really any other reason, is there? (He laughed, then assumed a more serious, obviously more comfortable, expression.) No, I wrote one of the first books in the series, and it seems to be doing all right, so they asked me to do another. That's all.

What was it called, the first one?

Roland smiled. *Radiant Brow.*

That's rather nice.

Oh, don't give me the credit. It's just a translation of the hero's name.

Jasmin sipped her beer. And what was that? she asked politely.

Taliesin. (His expression became almost stern. He obviously felt that he'd been put on the spot.) Taliesin is a kind of god, you see, a divine poet, a shapeshifter . . .

Shapeshifter? (She'd noted that he was using the present tense. She prayed that he wasn't going to be a crank.)

Well . . . He can assume different identities. His spirit keeps being reborn in different forms, from the beginning of time to the end of time. He's an absolutely central figure in Welsh myth.

Jasmin raised her eyebrows. So is the new book about this Taliesin as well?

No, but he's in it. You can't keep him out really. He gets everywhere . . . But look, it's okay. We don't have to talk about mythology.

That suited Jasmin fine. For an hour they talked about themselves instead. Jasmin found him pleasant company, down-to-earth, not crankish at all. It was reassuring to be asked a series of polite, straightforward questions about herself. She answered him readily. With a bit of editing here and there, she could still present her professional career in a fairly rosy light.

But she enjoyed hearing Roland talk about himself too. There was nothing too remarkable about him. He was a thirty-five-year-old teacher who wrote in his free time. He'd been married once, had no children, and lived in a flat out near the swimming pool.

His accent was vaguely rustic, perhaps Berkshire or Wiltshire, and he spoke about his own life with a strange detachment. He recalled dates and details with the meticulousness of someone who feared that one day all this information might be lost. Yet he managed to do it without any suggestion of arrogance.

I feel flush, he said eventually. Why don't we share a taxi home?

He squashed out a cigarette and looked straight into Jasmin's eyes. She'd noticed that he did this quite often, rather than averting his eyes, as a shy person might have been expected to do. It was a little disconcerting.

The night air was unseasonably cold. They had to walk some distance, Roland loping along on the curb side of Jasmin, before he managed to flag down a taxi.

During the ride home they talked mainly about music. Roland also told her that he was in the middle of a leisurely move, from his flat to a house six doors further up the same street. Jasmin felt pleased to have met Roland King. There really was something reassuring about him. Perhaps it was just the contrast with Lacy. But it felt good to be with a man who didn't set her nerves on edge, a man whom she could hope to gauge.

They swapped addresses and telephone numbers before the taxi stopped to let Jasmin out. She handed Roland some

coins toward the fare and he took them without any fuss
at all.

Jasmin stepped out onto the pavement. Roland shuffled
across the back seat and stopped her from closing the door.
She smiled down at him. They had already said goodbye.
What did he want now?

Look, he said, fixing her with those eyes, I don't want
to give you the wrong impression, but on the other hand
I don't see any point in messing around. I'm available. To
you. I'm available to you. That's all I want to say. (Still he
wouldn't look away.) I haven't offended you, have I?

Jasmin shook her head slowly. She was half expecting
him to laugh.

I'll see you, then, he said.

He slammed the taxi door and the driver moved off at
once. Jasmin stood outside her house for some time. One
of the neon lights was flickering in the window of the chem-
ists' opposite. Gusts of loud dance music reached her from
a house party further down the street. *I'm available*, she repeated silently to herself. *I'm available.* And it didn't after
all sound like such an extraordinary thing to say.

Roland King thus became available to Jasmin. And two
nights later, Lacy rang her and told her that he knew.

15

LACY RANG HER FROM A PAY PHONE.

Hello, my love, it's me, he said. I saw you the other night. Trying to get a taxi. I was going to stop and give you a lift. Then I saw you had company, like.

His voice sounded slurred, fruity. The line was bad. Jasmin shuddered. (Oh, God, oh, God, she thought.) Lacy, she said, I wasn't expecting to hear from you again. What do you want?

Want? I don't want anything, princess. I just saw you the other night so I thought I'd give you a ring. See how you were getting on. No harm in that, is there?

Jasmin shuddered again. She sat on the edge of the bed,

closed her eyes and tugged the hair at the nape of her neck. There was so much she wanted to say to him, ask him, accuse him of. She hardly knew where to start. (It occurred to her too that she hadn't even given Lacy her phone number. Had the boys given it to him? . . .)

I thought I saw you the other day, she began slowly. At the swimming pool. Wednesday afternoon. About half-past four?

Not me, Miss, he said at once. I've been out of town, see. On a job. Only got back at the weekend.

I thought you'd say something like that, said Jasmin.

Come again?

I said I thought you'd say something like that, she told him, more loudly. She was beginning to find her bearings now. Why did you just leave without saying anything when we came back from Wales?

Ah, he said, I remembered I had to be somewhere.

With your kids? At once Jasmin regretted saying that. She didn't want to sound bitchy. Not yet, not so soon.

No, as a matter of fact. Look, I'm sorry about leaving like that. Does it mean we're not friends any more?

We weren't really friends to start with, were we?

Jasmin hadn't meant to say that either. There was an uncomfortable pause. She could hear faint shouting at the other end of the line. Shouting and laughter. He was probably ringing her from a pub. Jasmin looked up at the truncated photo of her family. The photo which she'd vandalized in bed at St. David's.

My great aunt died, she said.

Died? Well there's unfortunate. Pleace accept my condolences.

He sounded sincere but not surprised. Had he forgotten what he'd said in the car outside the church. About death, about poor old Alice? Jasmin suddenly felt crushed. She couldn't take this any further on the phone. She needed to see his face. She needed to see his eyes.

Anyway, she went on, I saw my mother at the funeral. I gave her your present . . .

Did she like it? I hope she liked it.

She loved it. I . . . I'm not so sure what I thought though.

Oh?

Jasmin dipped her head. Lacy, how did you get all that detail into it? I mean, you only looked at the picture for a couple of minutes. Did you come to my room, when I was out, and take a photo of the picture or something? Please tell me the truth. It's bothering me. Please.

Jasmin's head was throbbing. She thought she could hear Lacy sighing quietly. He put in more money. But it was some time before he spoke.

I'm sorry I've upset you, he said. I really didn't mean to, love. You've got to believe that. You've got me all wrong. Really you have.

Jasmin picked up the phone and leaned against the window frame. She pinched the top of her nose in vexation. One of the boys was playing his acoustic guitar in the next room. She'd been so keen to talk to Lacy before this. So very keen. Quickly she began to mellow. I must get his number, she told herself, I must get his number so that I can reach him again.

I think, she told him at last, I think I'm just going through a bad patch. Things haven't been going the way I planned. I'm glad you phoned. Honestly. And I was most impressed with your carving. It was . . . well, it was magnificent.

Oh, God, no, Lacy laughed. It wasn't anything really. (He paused.) What did your dad think of it? And your sister?

I don't know. I don't know what my father thought. And my sister couldn't get back for the funeral.

Couldn't make it, eh? Well, there we are. So there wasn't a proper family reunion?

Jasmin closed her eyes again. What was it with him? *So it takes something out of the ordinary to bring you all together, then?* Now this.

I don't want this to sound petty, she said, But on the way back from Wales you said that you were "interested" in me. Did you really mean me—or my family? You just seem to *bring them up* so often.

If I'm interested in you, my love, he said at once, I've got to be interested in your family? Isn't that right?

Why? She tried to laugh but it sounded horribly false.

Well, because your family matters to you. It's there in that picture, in the look on your face. The minute I saw it, I thought: This girl's family matters to her. I could see other things too.

Oh, could you? Things like what?

Well, what can I say? Something not right between you and your father. Something not right between you and your sister. It's all there. Most people read books. I read photographs.

You're weird, Lacy, said Jasmin. (She knew that she'd lost any sort of initiative. What he'd said had been so right. So undeniably right. He was leading her again. Whether she liked it or not he was leading her again.) You say weird things. You do weird things. I mean, that weekend in Wales was, oh, I don't know, peculiar.

Peculiar? he repeated, laughing. Only because we didn't

sleep together. If we'd slept together you'd have thought it was all quite normal and healthy.

Jasmin caught her breath in astonishment. She wasn't used to this kind of exchange. She wasn't used to people telling her what she thought. Other people just took her so much more *seriously*.

What is it you want from me? she asked. Just tell me that.

Lacy laughed again, this time quite loudly. He was obviously having a whale of a time. I've got to go, he said. I'll be in touch—if you want me to be.

Give me a number, Jasmin said quickly, before she had time to think better of it. Give me a number where I can reach you sometime. Please.

Lacy reeled off a number straight away. Jasmin jotted it down on a scrap of paper under the photo.

Is . . . is there any time I shouldn't ring?

Oh, I wouldn't have thought so.

She read him back the number. He confirmed it, said goodbye, and put down the phone before she could say another word.

96

16

SO JASMIN HAD A NUMBER FOR LACY. THAT WAS SOMETHING. But she couldn't quite convince herself that it was a genuine one. She had a horrible feeling that he'd just dreamed it up on the spur of the moment. So later that week she gritted her teeth and dialed the six figures. To her relief and surprise a phone began to ring at the other end.

She replaced the receiver. At least for the time being she knew enough. The number existed. It might not actually be *Lacy's* number, but it did exist. The palms of her hands were moist. Her legs felt hollow. She didn't want to talk to him. Not yet. (She didn't really know what she wanted

to say to him.) But she knew that the time would come.
Soon.

At the weekend Roland rang. He wanted to take Jasmin
out to tea. Jasmin liked the quaintness of the idea, but she
had to say no. She'd already promised to visit a friend who
had given birth to a premature baby three days earlier. She
went on talking to Roland about nothing in particular. He
had an extremely relaxing telephone manner. Just listening
to his voice made Jasmin feel quite serene.

But the visit to the maternity hospital soon set her fret-
ting again. Her friend's baby had been born six weeks too
soon. Jasmin had visited special-care units once or twice
before, and she was prepared to be shocked. But this time
it was the sheer brute sadness of the place that got to her.
She stood poker-faced in the sweltering observation corridor, her eyes roaming over the lines of transparent cots
and incubators.

There weren't many parents in with the sick children.
Just a handful of young nurses and one strikingly handsome
pediatrician. Jasmin's friend was some distance away. She
waved, disappeared into a side cubicle, then came out and
held up a tiny, still bundle for Jasmin to see.

Jasmin smiled and nodded gamely. The baby couldn't
be brought to the window because it was being supplied
with oxygen through a short tube and funnel. Jasmin's
friend was smiling, utterly absorbed in her child. Her husband was with her. He looked exhausted, hunched in a plastic chair, drinking water from a paper cup.

Afterward Jasmin had a cup of coffee with both of them
in the hospital café. She'd bought the baby a present, a rub-
ber giraffe that squeaked and rattled. But she didn't give
it to them. At the time, it just didn't seem appropriate. They
told her about babies much smaller and sicker than their

own that had survived. They kept telling her how people had rallied round them. It was as if they were trying to reassure *her*. They didn't succeed.

Jasmin got drunk that evening. All by herself on a bottle of Valpolicella. Shortly after ten o'clock she rang Lacy's number again. For days she'd been struggling to work out why she needed to talk to him. Now she had capitulated. She listened to the ringing tone without the first idea of what she was going to say. She was aware that she might well find herself talking to his wife.

No one answered.

She drank some more wine and tried again fifteen minutes later. Before she could gather herself she was in conversation with a man. He had a thick, oafish voice, and he sounded as if he was just waking from sleep. He called her "mate."

No mate, he drawled, Tel's not here. I'll get him to give you a bell if he gets back, all right?

Yes, yes, said Jasmin quickly. Let me give you my name. She spelled out her name, slowly, loudly, even though she felt sure he wasn't taking it down. She also gave him her phone number, just in case Lacy had mislaid it since calling her before.

Can you tell me, Jasmin then asked, is this Lacy's home number or a friend's?

What's that? (He spoke like someone mimicking a complete idiot.)

Are you speaking from Lacy's home? Does Lacy actually live there?

There was no reply for several seconds. What do you mean, like? Do you mean does he live here all the time, like?

Jasmin snorted. Lacy! she said. It's you, isn't it?

There was another, longer, silence at the other end.

Lacy? . . . Jasmin said more tentatively. Come on. Stop teasing!

I'll tell him if he gets back, all right? (The voice was unchanged, completely deadpan.)

Jasmin's stomach lurched. She put her hand over her eyes. I'm sorry, she said, I thought you . . . I'm really sorry . . .

I'll get him to give you a bell. And he put down the phone.

Jasmin sat on her bed in silence until the boy in the next room began to make love to his girlfriend. Then she filled the space around her with radio music. She still had a niggling feeling that the oaf had been Lacy. Surely no one really spoke as moronically as that? But what had he meant by "if he gets back"? Where, or what, was Lacy supposed to come back to? Why was everything about Lacy so unnecessarily ambiguous?

He didn't ring Jasmin back that night. She tried his number again three times the following morning. The first time, just after eight, the line was engaged. The second and third times there was simply no answer.

Presuming that the oaf *hadn't* been Lacy, there was a chance that he'd forgotten to pass on her message. It was plausible. But Jasmin didn't really believe it. She was always ready to believe the worst about Lacy. Always. It was almost as if she was willing him to give her a hard time.

That Sunday afternoon she went swimming again. The weather was fine but she chose to go to the pool rather than the river. She didn't really expect to see Lacy there again, although he was obviously her reason for going.

The pool was less crowded than it had been the last time. Jasmin managed to complete twenty lengths. In a fit of high spirits she even made a couple of jumps from the high springboard. It was years since she'd had that sudden sensation of weightlessness, right out there above the water. It brought back all sorts of memories, not all of them bad or sad.

But Lacy wasn't there of course. Her eyes kept coming back to the spot where she'd seen him before. She remembered her fleeting glimpse so vividly. A good muscular back, good legs too. A small bottom. He'd have given her pause for thought even if he'd been a complete stranger.

It wasn't easy for Jasmin to admit this now. She'd convinced herself from the start that she didn't fancy Lacy. And when it came to men she'd always put an enormous amount of trust in her first impressions. Had she been kidding herself about Lacy before? Or was this something new, something to make the whole messy business even more confusing?

After she'd showered and changed she couldn't face the thought of going straight back home. (The boys had thrown a barbecue party that lunchtime. The garden would still be virtually out of bounds.) So she decided to drop in on Roland. He'd said he was going to be at home all weekend.

He lived somewhere in the warren of terraced streets that surrounded the swimming pool. Perversely, Jasmin could remember the numbers of both his flat and his house but not the name of the street. She started to cruise around the area, peering out at the street names, hoping that one of them would strike a chord. She wanted to see Roland. She really wanted to see him.

She found a street that sounded familiar. The houses were small, two-storied, and the gardens of those on the left ran down to the canal. Jasmin parked her car. The house in question looked very neat. Window boxes, freshly painted garden railings. There were two doorbells, one for the upstairs flat and one for the down. Roland's name was typed onto a sliver of paper that had been fixed next to the latter.

The front door was open. Jasmin tapped on it, tapped again, then walked inside. She called out but nobody came. The two main rooms had already been stripped of furniture. The kitchen was well stocked and clinically clean. Jasmin went to the window and looked out, thinking that Roland might be in the garden.

The garden was long and thin. It consisted mainly of a badly kept lawn. At the far end there was a shed, and next to it a white table and garden chair. It looked, to Jasmin, like the garden of someone who was rather lonely.

The kitchen door was open. She could hear voices, laughter, wafting up from the canal towpath. She craned her neck to see further along. She saw two people sitting on a backless bench. A girl and a man. The man had his arm around the girl's waist. Both were wearing swimming costumes. They were smoking cigarettes and looking out at the water.

The girl's long dark hair was straggly with wet. The man had no hair at all. This was no hallucination. The man was real, and he was quite definitely Lacy.

17

JASMIN HEARD FOOTSTEPS ON THE STAIRS AND TURNED.

Well, well. What a surprise!

It was Roland, in a tracksuit, holding a wicker basket full of dirty clothes. He took the cigarette from his mouth and kissed Jasmin on the cheek. It was a clumsy kiss. Jasmin guessed that he wasn't a practiced social kisser. They both turned to the kitchen window, almost in embarrassment.

It had started to rain. Lacy and the girl were still out there. Jasmin clutched the edge of the sink. She had to. The strength had gone from her legs.

I was at the pool, she told Roland as steadily as she could. I hope you don't mind me calling.

Roland laughed. He loaded his laundry into the washing machine, ran his fingers over the controls and then began to percolate some coffee. Jasmin couldn't move from the sink. There was a terrible tightening in her chest. She was breathing fast and shallow.

That guy out there by the canal, she said. Does he live around here?

Roland glanced out of the window. Him? He might do. I've seen him out there quite a bit in the last few weeks. Why? Do you know him?

I've met him. Once or twice. (Then, out of a strange mixture of bravura and helplessness, Jasmin felt impelled to tell Roland more.) His name's Lacy, she breathed, Terence Lacy.

Roland produced the equipment to make another cigarette. I had an encounter with him myself, he said. I was sitting down there by the shed and I saw him digging this hole with his hands. By the side of the towpath. I asked him what he was doing and he said he was planting nuts. Hazel nuts.

Did he say anything else? Jasmin asked. (She couldn't take her eyes off Lacy. He was hunched forward on the bench, feet wide apart, elbows on his knees. She'd never seen him smoking before. Somehow it made him look depressed, vulnerable. Jasmin wanted to be beside him. More than anything she wanted to be there in that girl's place.)

Oh, he told me plenty, said Roland. I couldn't get away. It was mostly about cars. He works in a garage, right?

A garage? Jasmin repeated, perplexed.

Well that's what he told me anyway. I liked him. Anyone who plants hazel nuts can't be all bad.

No, said Jasmin, I suppose not. She didn't know what else to say. But she knew what she wanted to do. She wanted to dash out of Roland's kitchen. She wanted to be down there at the water's edge, with Lacy, girl or no girl. In a twisted kind of way, she almost believed that Lacy was waiting for her out there.

This is dreadfully rude of me, she said, peeling herself away from the window at last, But I've got to talk to him. I won't be long. I . . . I'm sorry . . .

She broke into a skip half way across the lawn. The girl had gone. Lacy had risen, tossed away his cigarette butt, and was stretching. Jasmin was afraid that he was about to dive into the canal, away from her. She called out his name.

He turned his head in her direction after a slight but noticeable hesitation. His eyes were screwed up against the gusty rain.

You? was all he said. It was little more than a grunt. There was something quite ghastly about the way he looked. It was as if his body had been deflated. He was holding himself like an old man. An old man who has to plan each of his movements some way ahead. He was wearing a pair of ragged mauve underpants, not swimming trunks. And his penis wasn't completely flaccid. (Oh, God, thought Jasmin, Oh, God. I wasn't meant to see this. Not this.)

Jasmin went no closer than the foot of Roland's garden. Hello, she called out.

Lacy nodded and ran his hand across his face. He looked as if he hadn't shaved for days. Well, how about this, then? he muttered. He said the words slowly, without intonation, as though he were reading them from a board behind her head. Thirty yards or so up the canal, out of earshot, the girl was swimming in the dark water.

Did you get my message? Jasmin asked. I rang you.

A spasm of pain contorted Lacy's face. He looked crazy,

ferociously crazy. The girl was calling out to him. He paid no attention to her. What are you doing out here? he grunted. Jasmin had never seen or heard him like this before.

How do you mean? she said.

Here! Why are you out here talking to me? he almost shouted. Why aren't you in there? (He nodded at the back of Roland's house.) In there with your boyfriend?

Jasmin began to quake. There was such vehemence in what he'd said. Roland isn't my boyfriend, she said quietly. He's a friend, a . . . a colleague.

Hah! said Lacy. Hah! He rattled some phlegm up into his mouth and spat it into the rough grass at his feet. The girl had climbed out of the water on to the far bank. Jasmin couldn't make out too many details but she looked very young. Twenty perhaps. She was short and she had large round breasts.

The rain was building up to a steady drizzle. Is that your wife? asked Jasmin, nodding at the far bank.

What in hell are you talking about? said Lacy, staring, bemused, across the canal. You're always asking the wrong damned questions, he said. Always.

Jasmin, still quaking, swallowed hard. Thank you for telling me, she said softly. Look, I'm not going to make a scene. (It occurred to her later that she couldn't have made much of a scene anyway. Nothing had ever happened between her and Lacy to make a scene about.) Just let me know when I can see you again. Please Lacy. I know you're angry now. But I've got to see you. Really. When it isn't like this.

He scratched his neck. Jasmin watched his fingers moving delicately across his skin. What about him? Lacy asked, nodding again at Roland's house. Jasmin glanced over her shoulder. Roland was standing, watching, outside his kitchen door.

When she looked back at Lacy he was smiling a weak smile. I'll be there when you really need me, love, he told her. Then he drew himself up to say something brief, resounding, in his own language. He leered at her for several seconds before translating, or paraphrasing. What he said was this: In the day of trouble, I shall be of more use to you than three hundred salmon . . .

Jasmin shut her eyes tight. She couldn't believe that she was still standing there, in the rain, humiliating herself in front of two different men. But she was quite unable to walk away. She had to be with Lacy. She had to. Even when he was being foul, cruel, abusive, elusive. Even when he was wrapped up in another woman. For the first time in her life Jasmin stood stripped of her pride before a man.

Go well! said Lacy. And he twisted away from her, took two long strides forward, and dived gracefully into the water. Jasmin didn't wait to see him resurface. She walked down to where Roland was standing and went inside. Then, while Roland was pouring out the coffee, she began to cry.

18

ROLAND DIDN'T PRESS JASMIN, BUT SHE TOLD HIM A FAIR BIT about Lacy. She'd cried in his kitchen for so long. So quietly and so desperately. Now she felt obliged to give him some sort of explanation.

She told him how she'd met Lacy. She told him about Lacy's persistent interest in her family, about the carving he'd made for Eileen. But she said nothing about the trip to Wales. She wasn't prepared to tell him about that. Not yet. Roland listened closely, looking at her all the time, occasionally nodding his head or frowning. So what is it, exactly, that you want from him? he asked her eventually, Or is that a naive question?

Jasmin thought for some time before she answered. Her face felt stretched and raw from the crying. I'm not sure. Really I'm not. That's part of the problem. It's not . . . it's not at all simple. I don't quite know how to put it, but I've got this feeling that he's singled me out. Me and my family. It's starting to frighten me.

Singled you out? said Roland.

I . . . I've got an idea that he's *watching* me all the time, when I'm alone, when I'm with other people. He even told me he saw you and me the other evening, you know, when we were looking for the taxi. It's as if he's sort of circling me, stalking me . . . and in the end he's going to do something—probably something awful. And not just to me. I'm afraid he's going to do damage to my whole family. He keeps on asking these *questions* about them.

Roland shrugged. He didn't look as skeptical as he might have done. Well if he hasn't actually done anything yet, I wouldn't be inclined to worry about him. That's easy for me to say of course. You obviously know him better than I do.

I know him hardly at all, Jasmin said ruefully. I know nothing apart from what he's told me, and that could just be a pack of lies. I mean, he told me that he was a scaffolder. He told you he worked in a garage.

Perhaps he has trouble with the truth? said Roland with a smile. A lot of people do.

Jasmin passed her sodden paper tissue from hand to hand. She hadn't told Roland the whole truth herself. There were some things she couldn't tell another man. She couldn't tell him that almost from the start she'd been prepared to sleep with Lacy. She couldn't admit that now she was starting to want to sleep with Lacy. And she couldn't

begin to describe what she felt for that girl with the large
breasts, that girl who'd made Lacy's penis rise . . .

I'm all right really, she said. You must think I'm neu-
rotic, I can see that. It was just the way he spoke to me out
there. The way he was out there. He was like a completely
different person . . . And yet I can't say it was a total surprise. I'd already sensed there was someone like that inside
him. Someone dark, underneath all the talk and the bois-
terousness . . . (She stared at her coffee mug.) I suppose I
must have been scared of him from the start really.

Well, look, said Roland, If he gives you any more bother
why don't you give me a ring? As I told you before, I'm
available. I mean it.

Jasmin nodded. That's good of you, Roland. I appreciate
it. I'm so sorry about all this. I'm not normally so feeble.

Roland waved away her apologies. Would you like to
stay for something to eat? he asked. It wouldn't be anything
lavish but you're very welcome.

No, said Jasmin. No, I've got to be getting back. Some
other time though. Some other time I'd love to.

Well, how about Tuesday? said Roland at once.

Jasmin laughed. His perseverance amused her, pleased
her. Tuesday would be fine, she said. Thank you.

Jasmin drove the short distance to the end of the street.
Then she turned left into a gravelly pathway and parked.
The pathway led down to a bridge over the canal. The rain
was now very heavy. Jasmin took her umbrella from the
trunk and crossed the bridge on foot.

Neither Lacy nor the girl was anywhere to be seen. Jasmin began to walk along the muddy path on the bank. She
walked back toward Roland's garden, back to where she'd
seen them before. I shouldn't be doing this, she told herself,

I really shouldn't be doing this. I shouldn't be letting Roland see me doing this. But she kept on walking.

There were lights on in most of the houses across the canal. Jasmin looked hard into the bright kitchens and dining rooms. She was too far away to make out any people clearly. She kept on looking though. She looked at the toys and the bicycles scattered across many of the gardens. Family homes. Mothers and fathers were over there, thinking like mothers and fathers, planning like mothers and fathers. And all the children, the children, all those children . . .

She walked up as far as the next bridge then turned back. She felt exhausted yet oddly alert, too. Lacy was somewhere close by. She felt sure of that. Although she couldn't see him, she sensed that he had his eyes on her. Somewhere, somehow, Lacy was watching her every move. He was directing each move before she even made it. All the time. Day and night. Even when he had that girl with the breasts clambering on him, kissing him, reaching for him . . .

She drove straight back home, trying to pick herself up, trying not to feel nauseated by the thought of the girl. Kate wouldn't have let this happen to her, she told herself. She'd never have let herself go this far. (Kate had rarely told Jasmin anything about her men. Kate's men were just *there*. They usually did what she wanted them to. That was all there was to it. For Kate.)

Jasmin went up to her room and sat by the window. Her wine glasses were missing from the shelf. The boys had been in again. Half-a-dozen people were huddled under the shelter down on the patio. They'd had their barbecue regardless of the weather. Jasmin couldn't hear what they were talking about now but their voices sounded happy, happily drunken. She thought of ringing Roland, to apologize again. But instead she phoned her mother.

Eileen had just got back from church. She sounded unusually preoccupied. Kate still hadn't broken her news, the
news she'd said she was going to put in writing. Eileen had
been having all sorts of intimations. She felt sure that Kate
was either pregnant or ill, or both. Jasmin felt a twinge of
anxiety but she couldn't really share her mother's concern.
Kate didn't have problems like other girls, other women.

It that all that's worrying you? Jasmin asked. You don't
quite sound yourself.

No, no, said Eileen. There's nothing else. Nothing that
would interest you . . .

Oh, come on, Eileen. Tell me. (She tried to keep the
tension out of her voice. She was thinking, Don't let this
be serious. Please don't let this be serious.)

It's just that dream of mine, Eileen said slowly. That
dream I had before old Alice died. Well, the other night I
had it again.

Jasmin sighed to herself and kicked off her shoes. Do
you want to tell me about it? she asked. She knew that,
under different circumstances, Eileen would have been por-
ing over this dream with old Alice.

Oh, I don't know. You don't take it seriously, do you,
this kind of thing? You're always laughing at me . . .

Eileen, Jasmin said, if the dream is worrying you I want
to hear about it. Please.

It's not exactly *worrying* me any more, Eileen replied.
It's not really that. I mean, yes, when I had it the first time
I was scared. But now I'm not so sure. It's more confusing
now than anything . . .

She needed to be cajoled a little longer. But eventually,
in her own dramatic fashion, she gave Jasmin the outline of
her dream. Almost inevitably, it didn't sound as dire to
Jasmin as it had seemed inside her mother's troubled head.

Eileen was floating out at sea, alone, close to land. She could see a kind of cliff, and on the clifftop were the ruins of an old palace. A group of people was standing among the ruins. Sidney, Kate, Jasmin, old Frank, old Alice. They were standing very close together, as if they were posing for a photograph. They were near the edge of the cliff, with their backs to the water.

Eileen couldn't see a photographer. But she knew that he was there, beyond the ruins, and that he was going to make them all fall off, one by one. She tried to scream out a warning. No sound came from her throat. She screamed again and again but she couldn't make them hear . . .

Was that it? asked Jasmin, slightly uneasily. You must have got the idea of us standing together like that from old Frank's photo.

You don't understand about dreams, Jasmin, Eileen said wistfully. We have them for a reason. They're put in our heads to tell us things. Don't you see? Old Frank's picture might have set me *thinking* along those lines. But the picture's got nothing to do with the dream's message.

So tell me, said Jasmin, what was the message?

Eileen paused. That's what I'm not sure about. Obviously, the first time, I thought it was just a warning. A warning that something awful was going to happen, something to one of you. Or all of you. But then the second time it was different. You see, the first time I didn't actually see the photographer. But when I had the dream again, two nights ago, he came up and I got a look at him.

Really? Jasmin was beginning to feel distinctly queasy now. What was he like?

He was laughing. Not a nasty laugh. He wasn't frightening at all. And he didn't have a camera. But for some reason I kept on thinking of him as a photographer. He was saying something to the five of you. As if he was still lining you up, you know, to take a picture. He was smiling all the time. I stopped screaming then. I couldn't quite hear what he was saying, but I could make out his voice . . .

Well there you are, said Jasmin, who wanted to hear no more. I'm sure it isn't a warning or anything like that. Perhaps it means we're all going to get together soon. Something like that . . .

But the photographer, Eileen interrupted. That photographer . . . It might just have been because I'd been talking to you . . . And then there was the little carving . . . But the photographer sounded as if he was Welsh. And he had no hair. He was as bald as a coot.

19

JASMIN TRIED TO KEEP HERSELF BUSY OVER THE NEXT COUPLE of days. That Monday was fine so she drove to a village outside the city and had lunch in a pretty pub garden. Later she sauntered for a mile or two along the riverbank, exchanging the odd word with the men who were fishing.

In the evening she went to a film for the first time in months. In the lobby afterwards she ran into some friends, and went back to their house for a drink. It was after midnight when she got home. But she couldn't sleep at all. She could keep the lid on her anxieties for only so long.

She'd discussed Eileen's dream with her at some length. She'd also told her mother about her own dream, the one about the palace and the door. Eileen wasn't particularly bothered by the fact that a palace by the sea had figured in both dreams. Palaces, she said, were "quite normal." But she listened with great interest when Jasmin told her Lacy's story of the seven men and the forbidden door.

It's a bit like Adam and Eve, isn't it? she'd said. And Jasmin had supposed she was right. Adam and Eve. Pandora's box. Much the same idea, really.

There hadn't been a lot more to say. Jasmin didn't feel like suggesting that Lacy's carving might in some way be dangerous. She didn't have the words for it. Neither was she prepared to tell Eileen what Lacy had said about death, about old Alice. Not yet anyway. That would just have been too much. Yet Eileen had sounded so cool about the whole thing, so reasonable. And that in itself had unnerved Jasmin.

Now she lay fretful but motionless on top of her bed. It was stiflingly close in her small room. She'd been living in it for three years but she'd never quite thought of it as home. Never quite. Too much went on around that room that was nothing to do with Jasmin. It wasn't exactly an oasis yet it certainly wasn't a part of something bigger. And Lacy had been in there, too, without her, infecting it with his presence, making it even less of a home than it had been before.

Lacy. Always Lacy. Jasmin's thoughts curved back to him again and again. Her need to speak to him was more urgent than ever. His behavior beside the canal hadn't affected that urgency in any way. And neither had the girl. Neither had the girl . . .

She knew what Roland must have thought. That she was quite simply besotted with Lacy. Besotted to the extent that she could confront him when he was with another woman, when another man was watching. It must have seemed obvious to him. *What is it, exactly, that you want from him?* Roland had asked. *Or is that a naive question?*

Or is that a naive question? Oh, Roland had pigeonholed her straight away. He probably found her pathetic. A woman of her age, making a song and dance about some man who wouldn't give her what she wanted.

And in a sense of course he was right. Jasmin couldn't disguise from herself the fact that she wanted Lacy. She wanted him in just the way that Roland imagined. She wanted him in the way that the girl in the canal had had him. But there was more, too, much more.

She did feel that Lacy had singled her out. She *did* feel afraid that he was closing in on herself and her family. She thought of him as a liar, as a fraud, as someone who was, in some indefinable way, on the run. He wasn't her kind of man at all—not in the way that, say, Roland could be— yet there was something fearsomely compelling about him. Something that she was glad she'd never encountered before.

There just didn't seem to be any constructive way of thinking about him. *You're always asking the wrong damned questions,* he'd said. Perhaps he was right. Perhaps he really was right.

She spent most of the next day stopping herself from ringing Lacy's number. Roland phoned to check that she was still coming to dinner that evening. Jasmin said that she was, but part of her wished that she wasn't. This part of her wanted to say, No, after the scene by the canal I'm too embarrassed to eat food with you. But have you seen Lacy again? And what did he look like? And was he with that girl? . . .

At six-thirty she knelt beneath her window and rang

Lacy's number. The receiver was snatched up immediately at the other end. Jasmin winced. A child was screaming. Perhaps there were two children. A harrassed woman came on to the line.

Hello, hello, she said laughing. This is a bloody awful time to be calling! Sorry about the chaos. Who's there? . . .

Jasmin slammed down her receiver. The woman's voice had been mellow, middle-aged. Not a voice, Jasmin thought, that went with the body of that young girl in the canal. Not that sort of voice at all.

She felt giddy, sick, furious. She got to her feet and on an impulse she reached for the clay dragon. The dragon that Lacy had bought for her in St. David's. It was a ridiculous thing. Pot-bellied, lop-sided, ugly, poorly made, too distasteful even to be funny as kitsch.

Forcibly she dashed it to the floorboards of her room. It bounced, hit the side of her armchair and rolled, still intact, to a standstill. Jasmin stooped and picked it up again. This time she hurled it several feet across the room into her metal waste bin. It hit the inside with a dull ring then nestled down among the screwed-up papers.

It wasn't the best way to start an evening. But the dinner at Roland's turned out to have been a very good idea indeed.

To Jasmin's surprise, Roland had invited two other guests, a couple. The husband was an extremely funny Scotsman who ran a sports outfitters. His good humor was contagious. Jasmin drank more wine than she should have done as a driver, and gradually she began to relax for the first time in days. Roland's food helped, too. On the evidence of that meal, he was a quite marvelous cook.

Before the party broke up, they all went for a stroll along the moonlit canal towpath. The other couple walked on ahead, leaving Jasmin to talk alone with Roland for the first time that evening. But they said nothing to each other, nothing of any great weight or significance. And that was just how Jasmin wanted it to be. Roland seemed to have the precious knack of knowing what not to say. Even his idiosyncratic way of walking no longer bothered her. There was something, she thought, rather endearing about it.

They chatted on, mainly about films. Then at one point Roland guided her around a particularly wide puddle by placing a hand on her elbow. He left his hand there for longer than he really needed to. Jasmin knew what this was all about. Yes, all right, she thought. Yes, I don't mind at all. I need something uncomplicated. Something like this . . .

But although they weren't speaking about him, she couldn't help feeling that Lacy was around. In spirit he was there, between them, like a large and carefully wrapped present that they were both waiting to be allowed to open. It was surely inconceivable that Roland wouldn't want to know more about Lacy. Surely?

Back indoors, the other couple offered to drop Jasmin off on their way home. Roland urged her to accept. She was well over the alcohol limit and it was a reasonably long haul back to the other side of the city. He said that he would drive her own car over to her house on the following morning.

Jasmin eventually agreed to this. She didn't have the energy to argue with all three of them. Smiling, she handed her car keys to Roland.

Without any warning it had started to rain, hard. So while the husband went to fetch his car from the next street, Roland and his two other guests waited in the hall. A packing case full of books was standing under the coat rack. The wife dipped inside and produced a small beige-covered paperback.

Roland! she said in mock reproof. You never gave us our autographed copy!

Oh, said Jasmin by the front door, Is it the story you wrote about what's-his-name? . . .

Taliesin, Roland said dismissively. That's right. He seemed to be curling up inside his clothes.

Radiant Brow, the wife read out the title in a drunken declamatory style, *The Tale of Taliesin. Retold by Roland King.* . .

It's only a little thing, Roland said, buffing his glasses. You'd think it was rubbish.

With a playful smile the wife turned the book over. She began to read out the back cover text, her voice now low and husky:

> *I have been in many shapes,*
> *Before I attained a congenial form.*
> *I have been a narrow blade of a sword*
> *I have been a drop in the air.*
> *I have been a shining star.*
> *I have been a word in a book.*
> *I have been a book originally* . . .

She drew a breath and widened her eyes.

> . . . *There is nothing in which I have not been!*

Jasmin smiled. Roland reached out to take the book. Please, he said. This is awful. Come on, give it here.

But the wife swept it away from his grasp. . . . *This,* she continued, *is the classic story of Taliesin, the all-seeing, all-*

120

knowing poet god of the ancient Welsh. He comes to set prisoners free from ignorance, pride and despair. He comes to succor the unfortunate and to chastize the unworthy. He knows all wisdom. He will be, until the end of time, the liberator of the lost . . .

A car horn sounded out in the street. Roland looked mightily relieved. He's waiting, he said to the two women.

The wife passed the book across to Jasmin, who stared at it through an alcoholic haze. (The cover illustration, a simple line drawing, showed the infant Taliesin floating happily in a river full of salmon.) The phrase *liberator of the lost* echoed inside her head.

I want my autographed copy, said the wife before kissing Roland goodbye. It sounds good. Thrills and spills.

Yes, he sighed, turning to Jasmin, Plenty of those. He took the book from her. When she thanked him for the evening, he kissed her fondly on the cheek.

You haven't known Roland for long, then? asked the wife on the journey home. Jasmin shook her head. Ah, she went on. I don't suppose he's told you about his wife then?

He's divorced, isn't he? asked Jasmin, stiffening, although she wasn't entirely sure why.

Oh, no, said the woman. Sarah was killed. A drunk driver. She was on a bicycle. They kept her alive for two weeks but she wouldn't have walked again anyway. This was, oh, six years ago now.

Jasmin, sitting in the back of the car, didn't know what to say. The woman turned around and smiled at her. I hope you don't think I'm being morbid, she said, telling you that. I just think it's as well for people to know. Roland still keeps it to himself, you see. Do you know what I mean?

Jasmin nodded. For reasons that were quite outside her understanding, she was feeling close to tears again.

That night she lay awake for almost two hours before

falling asleep. There's so much cause for real grief, she kept on thinking, So much cause, and I'm *manufacturing* crises for myself. I ought to be ashamed. I deserve nothing. I deserve much less than I get . . .

She woke up soon after seven in the morning, her head teeming with a dream, that dream. She'd been back in the palace with the three doors. The light to either side of her, she now noticed, was sunlight, pouring in through two open doorways. There was a stillness all around her, a stillness that was slowly falling into fragments.

Then she could hear the voices, the sweet sad male voices. Louder now, more insistent. But were they urging her into the darkness ahead, toward the closed door? Or were they pulling her away, back into the light? Jasmin couldn't be sure of anything. But she felt happy. Childishly happy. She sensed that this was wrong. She was trying to remember just why she shouldn't be happy. It was no good. The singing swelled up. Jasmin was lost in the gorgeous melody, lost inside her own happiness.

It's happening now, said the single voice from nowhere, Lacy's voice, strangely distorted. You always knew it was going to happen. It has to happen to everyone. There's no need to be frightened. It's going to be all right. Trust me . . .

But when Jasmin awoke, all her fears and sadnesses came seeping back. And she longed to be asleep again, carefree, swamped in forgetfulness. But there was no singing around her now. Only the early morning shouts of the little girl in the next garden.

This is the day, she thought. Something's going to happen today. I can feel the danger. It's coming for me. It's coming for us.

And shortly after ten o'clock, Eileen rang.

20

It's about Kate, said Eileen. We got her letter this morning. Jasmin, the little madam's gone and got married.

Married! Jasmin almost shouted the word in disbelief.

It's hard to believe it, I know. A civil ceremony. Not a word to us. Not a word. They decided to do it just a couple of days before they went out and did it. It's so hard to believe. Your own daughter . . .

So who is he? asked Jasmin, still incredulous. Has she known him long or what?

Jasmin, I know about as much as you do. His name is Michael. That's all. Oh, and he works for his family's firm. Ceramics, whatever that means. Other than that she's told us nothing. Nothing. Not even his surname. And do you know why?

No. Tell me.

She's bringing him here at the weekend. She says she wants us to see him for ourselves. Form our own impressions. My God, Jas, she's a law unto herself, that girl! I just don't know what to think about it all. I mean, I'm pleased she's settling down and everything. But the way she's gone about it! Your father's not at all happy, of course. Well, you wouldn't expect him to be. He's always wanted to lay· on proper weddings, church weddings, for the both of you . . .

Is she pregnant then? Jasmin asked.

Eileen drew in her breath. Oh, Jasmin, she didn't say. I thought of that, of course. Well, you do, don't you? So did Sidney. I suppose it would explain a lot. We'll just have to see on Sunday. They're flying in at twelve, then taking a taxi from the airport. A taxi, mind you! He must be in the money.

There was a lengthy pause in the conversation. The news had made Jasmin feel quite light headed. But she had a pretty good idea what Eileen was going to say next. The suspense proved too much for her.

You're going to ask me to come back on Sunday, too, aren't you? said Jasmin.

Well, don't make it sound so outlandish, Eileen replied. It's not unnatural to want to have your family around you. You might realize that yourself one day. And anyway, you're the one who goes on about "a sense of family," remember? (Suddenly her voice changed, became softer, more persuasive.) You wouldn't have to stay for long, Jas. I'll make some lunch. They've got to get their plane back in the evening. It would only be for a few hours. And it would mean so much. So much.

Jasmin stared out of her window. The little mulatto girl was marching up and down the old man's vegetable patch. She was holding the sawn-off end of a broom handle in front of her, as if it were a microphone. Jasmin couldn't hear what she was singing, or saying. She was performing for her mother, a small dazzlingly white-skinned woman who was sitting on the lawn, reading a magazine.

You haven't been home for nearly six years, Eileen said. Six years! This is a grand opportunity to set things right again. I'll talk to your father. I'll make sure he doesn't step out of line. Go on, say you'll come. Say you will.

Still Jasmin said nothing. The white-skinned woman had noticed that Jasmin was looking down at her. She rustled her magazine, and abruptly told the child to keep quiet.

I don't know, Eileen, I just don't know, Jasmin said, turning away from the window. She glanced at old Frank's photo and looked away quickly. *So it takes something out of the ordinary to bring you all together, then?* She couldn't shake the words out of her head. There was no way that Lacy could have engineered this. No way at all. But the sheer persistence of the coincidences was unsettling her badly.

I don't know if this might make any difference, Eileen suggested, But you're welcome to bring your Welsh friend with you. We'd love to meet him . . .

Lacy! Jasmin cried. No, no I don't think that would be possible. I don't think that would be at all possible.

Well someone else then? Anyone, if it would make you feel easier about coming.

That gave Jasmin pause for thought. Slightly as she knew him, the first person who sprang to her mind was Roland. With Roland beside her, she might just be able to

125

face going back home. Amiable, available Roland, virtually a stranger. (But in a way, it *had* to be a stranger, someone who she'd never have to face again if it all went horribly wrong.)

And Jasmin had to go back. She had to. She'd have preferred a different context for the visit. But she knew that she had to go back sometime. So it might as well be sooner rather than later.

Well look, she said slowly, There is someone actually . . . (It occurred to her only then that she'd never mentioned Roland to Eileen.) He's, well he's someone I know through work. I don't know what he's doing on Sunday though. He's probably got something on. He's in the middle of moving house too. But I'll ask him. And if he's agreeable, then I will come, with him.

Having made even so qualified a promise, Jasmin felt quite debilitated. Eileen could scarcely contain her delight. She called it a "breakthrough." She talked about the family making a fresh start. She thanked God that Kate was bringing them all together again.

Jasmin listened, but she wasn't convinced. Kate just didn't seem to suit the role of peacebringer. What's happening to me? she thought. What's happening to my pride? A couple of weeks ago I wouldn't have dreamed of involving a person like Roland in a thing like this.

She looked out of the window again. The girl and her mother had gone. The make-believe microphone lay discarded on the path. The sight of it upset Jasmin. She was spending more and more time on the verge of tears. She knew that she had to get a grip on herself. She knew it.

At lunchtime Roland arrived in her car. I'm going to ask you to do me another favor, she said to him at once. Please don't say yes if you think you won't be able to face it. I'll understand perfectly. In fact you'll probably think I've got a terrific nerve just asking . . .

Get on with it then, he said with a grin. Shoot.

Jasmin sketched out what Roland needed to know, throwing in a little family history to put it into perspective. When she eventually invited him to accompany her home, it sounded like an offer which only a half-wit or a masochist could have accepted.

Of course I'll come, he said.

Seriously?

Oh, quite seriously. I'll be completely moved in and all together by the weekend. It'll be good to get away. There's just one condition.

Oh, yes. What's that?

That you come out to dinner with me on Thursday. How about Chinese?

Jasmin smiled. That's twice in one week, she said self-consciously. Are you sure? . . .

Roland just beamed at her.

So Jasmin found herself committed to going home. That evening she rang Eileen to tell her. But she'd forgotten that Eileen was visiting old Frank, and Sidney answered the phone.

I'm coming back on Sunday, she said. I'm bringing a friend. A colleague. His name's Roland.

So, said Sidney. Everyone coming home? We're very honored.

Jasmin bit her lip. What could she say to him? He sounded tired, morose. It'll be all right, Sidney, she said suddenly.

I know, Jasmin. I know . . . How is your work coming?

My work? Didn't Eileen tell you? I'm taking a break at the moment.

Oh? What, a week or so?

Well no, actually. It might turn out to be the whole summer.

He didn't reply at once. (On the rare occasions when they spoke calmly to each other, Sidney always asked about Jasmin's work. Jasmin had long ago realized that he did so as a substitute for asking her about herself. Now that she wasn't working, the main part of her had probably ceased to exist for him.) You know what you're doing Jasmin, he said, not attempting to disguise his bewilderment. You've got money?

Yes, she lied, I've got plenty of money. That's not a problem. I'll see you on Sunday.

Jasmin slept more soundly that night than she'd slept for some time. But again she woke up anticipating disaster. She wished that Sunday would just come and go and leave her to sort out her own dismal life.

But she still had to negotiate the rest of the week before Sunday. And that wasn't going to be easy as long as Lacy was around. Nothing was going to be easy as long as Lacy was around.

21

ON THAT THURSDAY MORNING ONE OF THE BOYS CAME TO SEE Jasmin in her room. The others had designated him to tell her that they were discussing a house party for the following Sunday evening.

The boys didn't entertain so spontaneously as a rule. They usually liked to have invitations printed and sent out several weeks in advance. Jasmin assumed that she was being presented with a fait accompli, and that therefore her own opinion was immaterial.

But she didn't feel put out. She couldn't afford to. I shall be away on Sunday, she said. I may not get back until late. By all means have your party. I hope it goes well.

The preparations began almost at once. The boys were awesomely thorough when it came to their pleasures. By Thursday afternoon, with Jasmin's consent, her room was being used as storage space for two armchairs and a rolled-up carpet from the lounge. The first guests began to arrive when Jasmin was taking a bath, before she was due to meet Roland that evening. They'd brought sleeping bags, and intended to bed down on the ground floor for a couple of nights.

I let too much happen to me, she thought as she dressed in her room. That's why I never get anywhere. That's why I'm always waiting, waiting . . .

But at least the upheaval in the house stopped her mind from running too often from Lacy to Kate and from Kate back to Lacy. At least there was that. But what about Kate? Jasmin thought in the bath, What *was* she up to? She didn't know what to think about her freewheeling sister getting married.

It was a shock, certainly. It was also a kind of declaration of a ceasefire, even though Kate herself would never have seen it in such terms. There had never been any direct rivalry between the two of them over men. The competitions, Jasmin had to admit, had all been held inside her own head. Even when they'd been at school, Kate had never shown a dangerous interest in Jasmin's boyfriends. In fact, Jasmin herself had always been more flirtatious with Kate's boys than Kate had been with hers. But Jasmin's suspicions remained, and rooted themselves ever more deeply. At the age of thirty-three, Jasmin still shrank from the prospect of a competition which she could never hope to win.

And now that Kate was married, Jasmin should have felt some sort of relief. But she didn't. She didn't. She just felt inexplicably cheated, and old, and nervous.

Roland, quite naturally, asked about Kate over dinner. He must have gauged from Jasmin's laconic answers that they weren't the closest of sisters. Quickly he shifted his line of questioning to her parents. And that, effectively, meant Sidney.

So how did he land up in England? he asked.

To tell you the truth, Jasmin replied, I don't know too much about what happened to him. He was in several different camps. One of them was actually in Germany. He's never forgiven the Germans. Apart from anything else, they killed two of his brothers and a cousin . . . Anyway, however it was that he got here, I don't think he was really intending to say in England. Then he met my mother, and then she got pregnant, with me . . . It happened pretty fast. He must have felt he had to stay.

And he never talks about it? The war, I mean?

No, said Jasmin, immediately thinking of Roland's own silence over his dead wife. He's a quiet man. I don't think he sees any of it in terms of words. It's still simmering inside him though—at least that's what my mother says. The only way he shows it now is with Germans. Any Germans. He still thinks of them all as the enemy. It's quite disturbing.

And quite understandable, said Roland. Anyway, he won't have to worry about me. I've got a bit of Irish in me somewhere but that's about it.

Oh, I'm sure he'll like you, Jasmin told him. (But already she'd wondered what Sidney was going to make of Roland. Already she'd realized that her own impression of Roland would be indelibly colored by that of her father. That was how it had always been with Jasmin. Kate, on the other hand, had never shown the slightest interest in Sidney's somewhat predictable opinions.)

Has he ever been back? asked Roland. To Warsaw, was it?

Quite a few times, yes. Just holidays. To begin with, we all went. I don't remember much about it now. Heat, and tiny flats full of people. Oh, and lovely ice cream. Not much else. Anyway Eileen—my mother—she couldn't stand it. She couldn't speak the language or anything. So Sidney took to going on his own. (Jasmin took a flap of the tablecloth between her fingers and kneaded it thoughtfully.) Every night that he was away, I used to pray so hard I thought I'd burst. I wanted God to make sure that he came back home again. I never thought he would, you see?

Surely they couldn't have detained him? I mean . . .

No no, not that. I was afraid that he'd *choose* not to come back.

Roland frowned. I see, he said. I see . . .

You don't, thought Jasmin, not really. You can't see that I'm still terrified, you can't see that I still pray to God to keep him here. You can't see what a pathetic, dreary, incompetent bag of nerves I am—otherwise you wouldn't be sitting there, would you? *Would* you?

Roland drove her back to her front door. He'd already said that he wouldn't come in for coffee. On the following morning he intended to finish moving. He wanted an early night and an early start. Jasmin appreciated his tact, because that was what it was. He was giving her some breathing space. She knew that if she insisted, only gently, he would come inside at once.

He was a good man. A really good man. She unfastened her seat belt and thanked him for the dinner.

I like being with you, Roland, she said unguardedly.

Obviously I liked being with you, too, he replied. His eyes seemed to be dancing behind his gold-rimmed glasses.

132

She leaned toward him and they kissed across the hand-brake and gear shift. It was uncomfortable but enjoyable. Roland was better at real kissing than he was at pecks on the cheek. After some minutes Jasmin pulled herself away, smiling.

I'll see you on Sunday, then, she said. And next week, I promise to read your story.

Oh! said Roland, Sod the story. I'd rather you spent the time with me.

Well, Jasmin laughed, climbing out of the car, Perhaps you should just read it to me then.

She watched Roland drive to the end of the street, waved, and let herself into the house by the kitchen door. At that point she didn't even notice the Volkswagen Golf which was parked opposite. Why should she have?

The kitchen was dark but there was a light on in the living room. Jasmin popped her head around the door. There were beer cans all over the floor. One of the boys' house guests was stretched out on the sofa reading a motor magazine. He was wearing a T-shirt and a pair of under-pants. The sight of that room depressed Jasmin instantly.

Hello, said the boy.

Hello, said Jasmin. Do you mind if I close the curtains? (She wondered afterwards what had led her to say that. She couldn't have cared less whether the curtains were open or closed. It could only have been latent house pride, a small pointless protest at what was happening in *her* house.)

She crossed the room. As she was tugging at the curtains she saw a flash of light out in the street. It came from behind a parked car, the Golf, a metallic-blue Golf.

Jasmin blinked, and she saw movement behind the car. A man, leaning across the car roof now, shuffling a camera into its case. She looked harder. She couldn't make out the man's face. Only the top of his head. He had no hair.

Jasmin cried out sharply and dashed from the living room into the hall. The front door wouldn't open. Some idiot had slipped the bottom bolt across. Furiously Jasmin worked it back then flung the door open.

She could hear the Golf's engine before she saw the car veering out into the street.

Stop! Jasmin yelled, raising her arm. Lacy!

The driver changed gear. The Golf accelerated away down toward the park. Jasmin was left standing at the front gate. She hadn't caught a clear glimpse of the driver's profile.

The boy from the lounge crept up behind her. He looked concerned.

You saw that, didn't you? Jasmin said, turning on him wild-eyed. You saw that car? He was taking pictures of the house! He was taking pictures of me in the house!

I saw a car . . . said the boy slowly, craning his neck to watch the tail lights disappear. Who was it? Someone you know?

I don't know, said Jasmin, putting a hand to her forehead, I don't know, I don't know.

She waited for half an hour and then she rang Lacy's number. No one answered for a very long time. Finally a man picked up the receiver and blearily recited the number. It was the oaf. Oh, my God, thought Jasmin, Oh, my Lord . . .

I'd like . . . to speak . . . to Lacy, she said, enunciating each word as if she was speaking to a child or a foreigner. This is Jasmin Piast. I'd like . . . to speak . . . to Lacy. Now.

Well he's not here, mate.

Jasmin suddenly wished she could reach down the

phone, grab this character by his throat and shake the truth out of him. When will he be back? she asked.

Sunday. He's away on one of those, you know, "musters" they call them. When all the soldiers sort of camp down for a bit together.

So he hasn't been here this evening? In the city?

Oh, no, no. He's been gone since yesterday. Up north it is, somewhere. I'll tell him you rang though, mate. I'll get him to give you a bell. All right?

Jasmin gripped the coil of phone wire. (She still thought that the oaf could be Lacy himself.) I don't believe you, she spat. I don't believe anything you're saying. I saw Lacy this evening! I saw him! Half an hour ago. And who are you, anyway?

What's that?

Who are you supposed to be? Lacy's minder or something? What are you doing there?

Me? Well I just live here. I'm a lodger, like. You know?

Oh! . . . Jasmin slammed down the phone.

She tried Lacy's number six times more during the two days that followed. Each time either the oaf or the mellow-voiced woman answered. Each time Jasmin replaced the receiver without speaking. I can't sink much lower than this, she thought after the sixth time, Please God, don't let me sink any lower than this . . .

But she still wasn't anywhere near the bottom.

22

I COULDN'T BE DOING THIS WITHOUT YOU, JASMIN SAID TO
Roland. Really I couldn't.

Roland smiled, kept his eyes on the road. They were
reaching the outskirts of Jasmin's home town and it was
gloriously sunny after some heavy showers along the way.
Jasmin felt jittery, sick in her stomach. She hadn't told Roland about the photograph incident. (She didn't intend telling Eileen either.) To keep her mind off things, she'd com-
plained lengthily to Roland about the boys at the house.
About the way they were encroaching too far on her life.

Why don't you move then? Roland said. There are
plenty of other places, better places.

Umm, said Jasmin. Umm . . .

They arrived shortly before one o'clock. Jasmin's parents' house wasn't unlike Frank's, at the other end of town. It had the same miniature quality, the same boxiness, even though it was semi-detached. Condensation was rushing off the hot wet pavement. Look, said Roland, pointing it out as he shunted the car into a space, Dragon's breath!

Eileen came out on to the pavement to meet them. Sidney stood on the front doorstep, wearing his charcoal suit and smoking a cigarette. Jasmin felt as if Eileen were lifting her bodily into the house, just in case her nerve should fail her at the last moment and she should flee back to the city.

There was a paper banner above the kitchen doorway. KATE AND MICHAEL, JASMIN AND ROLAND. WELCOME! it said. Kate had rung from the airport. Their plane had been held up, but now they were on their way. They were expected at any moment. Sidney fetched an unlabelled bottle of brown vodka and filled four thimble glasses. They drank, standing in the living room, to "the family."

Something out of the ordinary, thought Jasmin, looking around her. *Something out of the ordinary.* The table had been laid. Paper serviettes. The TV set had been pushed back against the French windows. An armchair from the front room had been placed in front of it. There was hardly any free space left at all.

So Jasmin was back in her home. She'd been unhappier within these four walls than in any other place in the world. Now what? she thought with mounting trepidation. Now what? And she knew that the giant's hand was closing on them again.

Sidney invited Roland to come out and inspect his garden. They took the vodka bottle, and two fresh glasses. Jasmin followed Eileen into the kitchen. There was food everywhere. Salads in bowls covered in plastic wrap, plates of cold meat, thinly sliced bread and butter, trifles. Sidney had made one of his large cheesecakes. Lacy's sandalwood carving was standing on the windowsill.

Eileen reached for it. I had my dream again last night, she said with a coy little smile. (Jasmin looked at her aghast. Her mother was holding the carving up to her cheek with one hand and stroking it with the other.) I'm not in the slightest bit worried now. Not in the slightest. It's all going to be all right. You see, the photographer did make you all step further and further back. You reached the very edge of the cliff. And then you just floated up into the air! All of you. You didn't fall at all! You were up there, above me, all five of you, and each one of you was looking so *happy* . . .

Jasmin stared at her mother with a kaleidoscopic expression on her face. Eileen was still fondling the carving. Why are you doing that? Jasmin asked. What are you doing with that bit of wood?

Eileen smiled the smile of someone who knows. Someone who knows, and feels pity for those who are still ignorant. This little thing, she said. This little thing has made me so happy. I take it around with me all the time. I show it to people. It just makes me feel so good.

Well I don't like it, Jasmin said bluntly. It frightens me. It's like a sort of ritual thing. I think you should get rid of it.

Eileen looked at her as if she were mad. You worry much too much, she said. You always have done. Believe me, Jas, everything's going to be all right. In the end, it's going to work out fine. For all of us.

They both turned and looked out the kitchen window. The two men were sitting outside the shed, drinking and smoking, looking rather splendid in their suits. He looks like a good man, said Eileen. Your Roland, he looks like a good man . . .

And then Kate and Michael arrived. And at once Jasmin knew that the danger was imminent. Real danger. The sort that could rip the beating heart out of a family.

Kate had grown her hair out. She looked marvelous in an expensive fawn-colored blouse and black jeans. She kissed Eileen, Sidney, and Jasmin, and shook hands with Roland. If she really was pregnant, no one could possibly have guessed.

Michael wasn't exactly what Jasmin had been expecting. He was probably in his late twenties, and attractive in a small-featured, pretty sort of way. Jasmin had always imagined that Kate would settle for a much older, suaver man. This Michael seemed rather gauche. Either that, or he was phenomenally nervy. One thing about him was certain though—he wasn't English. He spoke softly, willingly, yet Jasmin couldn't quite place his accent.

They moved en bloc into the living room. They stood in a ragged circle, drinking more vodka, while Kate described how she and Michael had met. Apparently they had known each other for quite some time. And Michael must have been "in the money," as Eileen put it, because Kate had given up her job. Jasmin carried on listening, but she wasn't taking it in.

She looked from face to face. She looked at Eileen, clutching Lacy's carving to her breast. She looked at Sidney, taking out his pack of cigarettes and offering one to Roland. None of it seemed real. None of it seemed as if it could possibly last. She began to panic. She saw Lacy's face again, the way he'd looked at her beside the canal, leering, lowering. *In the day of trouble* . . . Lacy, she said to herself, Lacy don't do it. Please don't do it . . .

Well all we want to say is this, said Eileen. (Jasmin could see that she'd prepared some lines, and they all came out in a tumble.) Welcome to our family, Michael. We're delighted for Kate, for both of you. We're just ordinary people, but what we have is yours, we mean that . . .

She glanced at Sidney before continuing. And if . . . and if you didn't mind, we'd like to have a little party here sometime. Sometime soon. Just for the two families. So we could get to know each other. Nothing grand. We know Kate doesn't go for anything grand. But we could invite the minister from our church. It's a Baptist church, Michael. I'm sure you had your reasons for getting married as you did. But we'd like it so much if our minister could, well, bless your marriage. Anyway, that's . . . what . . . we . . . were . . . wondering . . .

I think that's a fine idea, Michael said graciously. We'd love to do that, wouldn't we, Kate? (Kate nodded, but she looked drained, tense.) I've got to come over from Brussels again in two week's time. Business, you know? Would that be too soon? I'm sure my people would be able to come then.

Oh, that would be marvelous, said Eileen. Marvelous! . . . So, so where is it that your people would be coming from, Michael? I'm sure you don't mind me asking—Kate didn't tell us, you see—but you're not English, are you?

No, Mrs. Piast, Michael replied, glancing at Kate. That's right. I'm not.

You're from Belgium, then?

In point of fact, no. He glanced at Kate again. He looked

seriously distressed. Jasmin closed her eyes. This was it. This was going to be it.

As a matter of fact, Kate herself said at last, with all her lovely features drawn forward on her face. As a matter of fact Michael comes from Frankfurt.

Frankfurt? Eileen's face was caught between a smile and a look of terror.

You know, said Kate, Frankfurt? West Germany. Our side.

Eileen grinned deliriously at Michael because she couldn't bear to look at Sidney's reaction. But Jasmin was looking at Sidney. Jasmin saw it all.

He'd been in the middle of lighting a cigarette. Impenetrable behind his cupped hands. He finished the job, and threw the match into the grate. He was looking at the ceiling, blowing smoke at the ceiling.

No one could say another word. Excuse me, Sidney muttered. He backed away, eased himself around the furniture, and disappeared into the kitchen. Moments later, he reappeared in the garden.

Kate had taken hold of Michael's arm and buried her face in his chest. Eileen stood motionless, all expression wiped from her face. Kate had really done it. She'd married a German. She'd married into the forbidden nation, and she'd brought her German husband under Sidney's roof. Jasmin smiled at Roland. I'll go to him, she said, I'll go to him.

23

SIDNEY, SHE SAID. SIDNEY.

He was standing on the lawn, one foot on either side of the hole in which Eileen planted the pole of her revolving washing-line.

Sidney . . .

Jasmin knew that the others were watching through the French windows. Sidney kept his hands at his sides, his cigarette clenched between his lips. He didn't look furious. He didn't look mortified or humiliated. He just looked what he was—implacable, unreachable, a man from the camps, a man who hadn't been expecting to survive but had gone on to live for a further forty years inside the echo of a life that had screamed itself out.

Jasmin couldn't compete with Sidney's history. None of them could.

Sidney, is there anything I can say?

Sidney looked ahead of him, across the row of little English gardens. So neat, so contained. Under his breath he was murmuring something. He was speaking in his own language.

Shall I ask Kate to come out? That must be why she brought him here. To explain. She's your daughter. You've got to let her explain . . .

He murmured on. He wasn't a melodramatic man. What he was saying was coming from the heart. Jasmin had to respect that. The sun was high and hot but Jasmin was shivering. Why does this have to happen? she thought, Why does this kind of thing ever have to happen? Who makes it happen? But already she sensed an answer that she hardly dared to acknowledge.

Sidney walked across to his shed. He fished the key from his trouser pocket, unlocked the door, and went inside. Jasmin walked slowly back to the house.

Eileen was in the kitchen, dishing up food.

We'll just go on as normal, she said in her businesslike way. We've got guests. We've got to go on as normal. Kate's upstairs. She's in a state.

Jasmin saw Lacy's carving. Eileen had placed it beside her on the kitchen counter. Jasmin put out a hand and touched her mother's elbow. Eileen simply stared back. Out in the hallway, Roland was speaking with Michael. From what Jasmin could hear of it, he was talking the young German out of going to see Sidney and accounting for himself in person.

He's in the shed, Jasmin said quietly to her mother. Go and talk to him. Please. I can't think of anything to say. I can't get through to him.

Eileen took a deep, deep breath. Her face seemed to be pumped up with frustration. Utter, all-consuming frustration at the way in which her entire life had been closed off by the wrong choice of husband. There's nothing I can say to him, Jas, she said without detectable regret. I've never understood him. He's never understood me. There's just no love between us. Not now. Not for a long time.

Jasmin gaped at her mother. These weren't the sort of words she associated with Eileen. Not the sort of words, not the sort of sentiments. Eileen had always been the one who'd reassured her. The one who'd told her not to fret about the family rows. The one who'd been a walking, talking guarantee that the family would hold together. Jasmin gaped at her and she saw no bitterness, no resentment, only relief, resignation.

And so Jasmin had to go out to Sidney again. She walked down to the shed. The door was locked. She shook the handle, calling his name, telling herself not to cry. Then she peered through the cobwebbed window. It was hard to see anything inside. But she peered closer, and she glimpsed the back of Sidney's head.

Then, shielding her eyes from the sunlight, she made out the rest of him, inside his good charcoal suit. He was splayed out on the filthy floor, his face jammed tight against a watering can.

Jasmin screamed. She screamed for Roland.

Roland came running. He took one look through the window then kicked down the door. And then, because no one else seemed able to move, he rushed indoors to telephone for an ambulance.

Death's just a means to an end. Death's just a means to an end. The words chased round and round inside Jasmin's head. Eileen was beside her now, still fiddling with her carving. The carving which didn't show Sidney. The carving which showed Eileen but didn't show poor Sidney.

I wish you'd throw that bloody thing away, said Jasmin in a distracted whisper.

Eileen didn't hear her. She knelt down and cradled her husband's head in her lap.

Oh, Christ, Kate was saying, her face smeared with tears, Oh, Christ, don't let him die.

Jasmin looked at her venomously. It's not up to Christ, she said.

24

SIDNEY DIDN'T DIE. IT WAS JUST A MILD STROKE.

The three women got back from the hospital at six-thirty. Michael was needed back in Brussels that evening. So he'd taken a taxi to the airport as soon as he knew that Sidney was going to be all right. Roland had stayed at the house. He made coffee for the women and poured a glass of brandy for each of them.

They sat quietly in the kitchen, surrounded by the debris of a day gone wrong. How long are they going to keep him in? asked Roland.

They can't say, Eileen told him. Not for certain. A day or two, just for observation.

But at least he's going to be all right?

Oh, yes, said Eileen. Everything's going to be all right.

And completely without warning she began to chuckle. I don't know why I'm laughing, she gasped. Really I don't. You must think I'm awful.

Kate produced a pack of cigarettes. She offered it to Roland. They both lit up. Jasmin looked at them across the kitchen counter and wished that she smoked too.

Would you rather I left the three of you alone? asked Roland. So that you can talk?

Eileen shook her head good humoredly. There's nothing we can say, my dear. (And Jasmin realized that she was right. They'd said virtually nothing since Jasmin had screamed for Roland in the garden. Perhaps their feelings surpassed or fell short of the need for words? They all knew where they stood. They all knew what they thought of each other. Words just weren't necessary.)

Kate was going to stay on with Eileen, at least until Sidney came home, and possibly for the full two weeks until the party. Eileen was still intending to have her party, regardless of what had happened. Jasmin and Roland had a small meal, then prepared to leave just before eight.

I like Roland, Eileen whispered to Jasmin as she helped her into her jacket. I like him a lot.

Good, said Jasmin indifferently. Are you sure you're going to be all right? (She couldn't believe that her mother was going to remain so stoical, so untouched by it all.)

I'll be fine, Jas. You can't wish these things away. They're meant to happen, one way or another. I'll keep myself busy. And I'm definitely going to have that party, you know. Your father can do what he likes. I'm going to have it. You'll come, won't you.

Jasmin hesitated. Roland came out of the kitchen.

You'll bring her, won't you, Roland? said Eileen. Two weeks today. It's . . . important that we have it, and that you all come. It'll make up for today. I'm so sorry we've put you through this, Roland. So sorry . . .

Roland kissed her before leaving. He shook Kate's hand. Jasmin felt desperately weary as she got into Roland's car. She was too tired even to add her own apologies for the disastrous day. All she could see was Roland lugging Sidney out of the shed, and the walls of that hospital waiting room, and the succession of unwanted cups of tea. After ten miles or so she fell sound asleep.

The first thing Roland said when she woke up was, It'll be all right.

She wanted to cry but she felt too exhausted and un-comfortable. I mustn't start talking about Lacy, she thought. I can't afford to. I've got to stop thinking about him. I've got to.

What did you think of Kate? she said instead.

I thought she was almost as gorgeous as you.

Pah! said Jasmin, staring out into the night. I used to think Kate was lying in ambush for me, waiting to steal the most important man in my life.

Who was this man?

Someone I never met, said Jasmin. And then it dawned on her that she was going to walk right into the boys' house party when she got back. She reminded Roland.

It might be just the thing for you, he said. Stop your brooding.

Jasmin raised her eyebrows at him. Roland, she said, I really don't think I can face it.

Roland kept his eyes on the road. Well, stay at my place then, he said. He sounded impressively neutral about it.

148

Jasmin searched his profile. I'd like to, she said. I'd like to very much.

They traveled on in silence for a few moments.

Is it all right if we stop off at the house though? she said eventually. I'll have to collect a few things. (She was thinking, primarily, of her diaphragm.)

When they reached the house it was swarming with smart young men and women. They all stepped aside politely to let Jasmin and Roland pass. It had started to rain, so there were more people indoors than there should have been. Jasmin picked her way up the stairs. She expected to find people in her room. It was always impossible to keep them out.

Sure enough, she had to knock before she could enter. Someone in a chair was blocking the door. The room was illuminated by a single low lamp. Jasmin could see at a glance that nothing had been disturbed. Everything still stood as she had left it that morning. Except for one thing. The horrid little dragon had been taken from the waste basket and put back in its original position on Jasmin's music center.

There were people in each of the three armchairs. There were more people sitting on the bed. Jasmin's head began to swim. She knew that he was there a split second before she saw him. Lacy! Perched on the edge of her bed, dressed in his Cavalier uniform. And next to him, with his arm around her waist, a woman.

Not the big-breasted girl. Not her. But an angular-featured, sallow-skinned woman who was well into her thirties. And who was also, as far as Jasmin could see, about five months pregnant.

So! cried Lacy, raising a beer can to Jasmin. My princess has come!

149

25

THE SIGHT OF LACY WRENCHED SOMETHING FREE INSIDE JASMIN. Something she'd been struggling with ever since Kate had said what she'd come home to say. Perhaps for longer than that—much, much longer.

For an endless moment she stared into his face. It was flushed and mobile with drink. She looked down, saw the pregnant woman's elbow and forearm resting along his thigh. Then she lunged forward and slapped Lacy hard on the side of his head.

Immediately the room was in chaos. Lacy cried out in alarm, the pregnant woman shrieked, the other party guests jumped to their feet. Roland was behind Jasmin, pulling her

away from the bed. Jasmin herself was crying uncontrollably, trying to shake Roland off, shouting *You! You!
You!* . . . at Lacy on the bed.

And in that brief period of chaos, Jasmin loathed and
feared and wanted Lacy more than at any time in her life.
Even through her own hysteria she was aware of the wanting. Even as she shouted she was thinking, Why does Roland have to be here? Why does Lacy have to see me with
Roland again?

Then she saw the bemused expression on Lacy's face.
She saw his eyes. Those two deep shadows, coaxing her
into silence, into surrender. She sobbed helplessly, allowing
Roland to pull her towards the door by her waist.

She's had a hell of a day, she heard Roland announcing
to the astonished room. Her father's had a stroke . . .

At that she thrust his arm away. *Don't you dare talk about
my family!* she shouted. *Don't you dare! Don't you ever!*

She stood unsteadily near the door, her eyes blazing over
Roland and then over Lacy, who was still on the bed. Lacy.
She wanted to sink herself in him. Still, still. Nothing had
changed. She scorched the rest of the room with her gaze.
Everyone, everything. Her room. The only room in the
world that was completely her own. This was all she had
after getting up and going to bed for nearly thirty-four
years.

Your things, Roland was whispering behind her. Can
you just get your things and we'll go?

I don't need anything from here, she thought. But then,
as if to correct herself, she brushed past a middle-aged man
who was smoking a cigar, to get to the bulletin board. She
unpinned the photo of her family and pressed it flat against
her breast.

That was enough. She didn't even look at Lacy as she

wheeled around and left the room. He could have the rest. It was his now anyway. He'd loaded it all with himself. He'd tarnished it all beyond recovery.

A small crowd was standing quietly on the landing, alerted, eager to see what was going to happen next. Jasmin pushed her way through to the stairs, closely followed by Roland.

Oh, God, Roland, she said when they were back on the ground floor, I don't think I ever want to come back here again.

But the loud music drowned what she'd said. And when Roland leaned closer and asked her to repeat it, she simply shook her head and led the way out to the car.

On the journey across the city Jasmin stared fixedly at the photo in her lap. Four mournful faces. Four lost souls. The giant had them in his fist now. The giant could do just what he liked with them.

But how on earth had Lacy come to be at that party? Who had told him about it, him and his pregnant woman? And she knew she shouldn't have hit him. It had been a mistake. A bad mistake. In front of *her*. In front of the boys' friends. In front—oh worst of all—in front of Roland again.

Yet why didn't Roland ask her anything about Lacy? Why didn't Lacy seem to matter to him at all? Why didn't Roland give her a chance to explain herself to him? All he could do was drive and smoke and nod his head in time to the music on the radio.

I'm sorry I screamed at you back there, said Jasmin. It wasn't you I was angry with . . . But why don't you ask me? she went on, close to petulance. About Lacy? I won't mind.

I don't ask, Roland said carefully, Because quite honestly, I know as much as I need to know about him. It's something you've got yourself into. I'd prefer it if you got yourself out of it. I think you'd prefer it too. I'll do anything I can to help, of course . . .

They traveled on in silence.

I don't mean to sound smug, said Roland after a while. I suppose I'm just lazy about getting worked up. I'm sorry if that bothers you.

It's not what you think, Jasmin said at once, ignoring what Roland had told her. It's not what you think at all between Lacy and me. I know what you must think. I do. But honestly I feel he's doing something to my life. He's hitting me all the time where I'm most vulnerable. I can't say how he's doing it exactly. I can't say *why*. But I'm scared, Roland, I'm really scared . . .

Roland sat back and put his arm around Jasmin. You're tired, he said. You need sleep.

Jasmin slumped in her seat, close to despair. I need a hell of a lot more than sleep, she thought.

But by the time Roland was ushering her up the stairs of his fine new house, Jasmin felt as if she could sleep for weeks. There was still a lot of decorating to be done. But already the house bore Roland's imprint—a rich, unpretentious kind of tranquility. I could sleep properly here, thought Jasmin, I could wake up here without panicking.

Roland showed her to the smallest bedroom, where a wide single bed was already made up.

Where will you be? asked Jasmin.

In there, said Roland, pointing to the bedroom at the front of the house.

Jasmin followed him back downstairs. She phoned Eileen from the kitchen, just to make sure that there had been no further complications. Eileen sounded very buoyant. She said that Sidney's condition had improved, that he wouldn't have to stay in the hospital much longer. She thanked Jasmin for being there that day, Jasmin, and Roland, too.

Jasmin, for her part, didn't mention that she was spending the night away from home. It wasn't any of Eileen's business. That kind of thing should never have been Eileen's business in the first place.

When she'd finished her call, Roland asked her if she wanted a nightcap. Jasmin asked him for a brandy. He had to go and find the crate with his supply of alcohol in it.

Jasmin sat at the kitchen table and waited. Roland seemed to be gone for a long time. There were stacks of books all over the kitchen floor. She thought of Roland's unread typescript, back there in her own room. (*Her own room.* The words sounded so inapplicable now.) I must read Roland's story, she told herself. It's the least I can do, the least . . .

Absently she laid her photo in front of her, then picked up a pen and drew two little horns, very close together, on top of the visible section of Kate's head.

Roland returned with a bottle of cognac. He looked over her shoulder.

What a strange little photo, he said. You look nice though.

No I don't, said Jasmin. I look pregnant.

Roland looked closer. You've put horns on Kate? he said.

Jasmin nodded. She knew that she was going to cry.

Roland put his hand on her shoulder. Is that how you feel about Kate now? he said.

Jasmin pursed her lips. The tears were coursing down her cheeks.

Roland poured out two large measures and they drank

them where they were—Jasmin at the table, Roland standing next to her, holding her head against his thigh.

Jasmin pushed her empty glass away, stood, and embraced Roland. He kissed her back, keenly. Jasmin plucked his glasses from his face and played her fingers around his eyes.

I'm not sleeping on my own tonight, she told him.

Roland smiled. You're the boss, he said.

No I'm not. Really, I'm not . . . And they kissed again.

So Jasmin went to bed with the man who'd declared himself available to her.

They made love like two people who weren't in any hurry. Roland was a generous lover, but he couldn't make Jasmin forget. And before it was over, she had the same semidelirious vision that she'd had in St. David's: Lacy, standing naked at the foot of the bed, pointing his penis at her like a shotgun, black wells of nothing where his eyes should have been. But this time he was smiling.

Then Jasmin held Roland against her through a long and wakeful silence. They had made love without taking precautions.

Jasmin's diaphragm was still there at the house. It was part of the luggage which she'd decided to leave behind. She'd brought her picture but she'd left her diaphragm. It hadn't been an oversight. She'd known, and she'd gone ahead—with Roland. It had just seemed the thing to do. With Roland . . .

Jasmin felt a long way from anywhere that night. She felt safe, but she knew that this was only a reprieve. Unless she were to be with Roland—or someone like Roland—for scores of nights like this, hundreds of nights, it would only ever be a reprieve. And she didn't honestly know whether

she was ready for more than that yet. She didn't honestly
know.

They slept until late the next morning. Roland cooked
breakfast. Jasmin sat at the kitchen table studying her truncated, and now defaced, photograph. It was a sobering
sight. So much had happened in so short a time. Old Alice
gone, Kate playing havoc with Sidney, Eileen drifting into
a domestic form of mysticism, and herself . . . What of
herself? What of Jasmin?

She's lost her dignity, and she'd gained Roland. I've lost
all my dignity, she thought, watching Roland eat his breakfast, And I've gained you. If Lacy hadn't still been there,
presiding over the disintegration of her life like a toast-
master, it mightn't have seemed a bad bargain.

But Lacy was still there. Jasmin couldn't just step out
of his shadow. She couldn't, and she didn't want to.

Roland suggested that she should stay with him that
day. He'd got some ideas about what they might do together. Jasmin backed off. It wasn't easy. There was such
serenity in Roland's house. The whole place seemed to be
pleading with her to stay.

I need a bit of time, she said. This is happening very
fast. Everything's happening so fast. Would you give me a
few days? Just to myself?

Roland smiled. He had the sort of face that scarcely registered disappointments. When they'd finished breakfast, he
drove her back to her house. Jasmin asked him to come up
to her room with her. She wasn't quite sure what she was
afraid of. But she didn't feel confident about going in on
her own.

The boys and their house guests were busy clearing up
the party mess in the kitchen. They said hello amiably
enough. They said nothing about Jasmin's performance of

the previous evening. (What could they have said? To her? They'd probably been laughing about it all morning. A thing that had happened at a party. A scene. A story for later.)

I've got to get out of this place, Jasmin told herself as she climbed the stairs, I've got to leave these people behind. And then it came back to her with a jolt: I didn't use my diaphragm last night. Why didn't I use my diaphragm? Why did it seem so right not to use it?

Her room looked undamaged. It was as if nothing had ever happened in there. Even the duvet had been smoothed over where Lacy had been sitting. But the room was thick with him. Him and his little dragon, up there on the music center. Jasmin pinned her photo back on to the bulletin board, then threw open the window to get some air circulating.

For a moment she stood transfixed. The woman next door was out in the garden, holding the little girl by the arm and smacking her on the bottom. It made a curious scene, since neither of them was uttering a sound. Then the girl fled indoors, and the woman remained where she was, staring out at nothing.

Roland put his arms around Jasmin from behind. He saw the woman. Petite, dark, quite pretty.

Do you know her? asked Roland.

No, said Jasmin thoughtfully. She doesn't live there. She comes to stay with the old man, for weeks at a time. She always brings the girl. I've never seen a man, a husband. (Jasmin rested her hands on Roland's.) I think she's lucky.

Why?

Oh, I don't know, said Jasmin, turning into Roland's arms, Perhaps because she's got her daughter. And her daughter's got her. And they seem so . . . sorted out.

157

They kissed and the phone began to ring. One of the boys took it downstairs. It's for you, he called up to Jasmin.

I'd better be going, said Roland.

Jasmin picked up her receiver. No, she told him, Don't go yet. She had an awful feeling that this was going to be about Sidney.

I'm returning your call.

It was a man's voice, clipped, impatient. It was Lacy.

Jasmin said nothing. She looked across at Roland, who had his hand on the door. Shall I go? he mouthed.

Jasmin closed her eyes, nodded, and put her hand over the mouthpiece. I'll ring you, she promised him, I'll ring you.

And Roland smiled, then left the room, closing the door behind him.

26

I'M RETURNING YOUR CALL, LACY REPEATED, LESS ABRUPTLY this time. You rang me when I was away on the muster.

There was a sudden constriction in Jasmin's throat. Her tongue wouldn't seem to work. Lacy, she said, Lacy . . .

It was Lacy who broke the silence that followed. Look, he said, I was sorry to hear about your dad. Really. People get over strokes though. I mean, he's a fit man as a rule, isn't he?

I don't . . . said Jasmin, I don't think I can talk to you any more about my family, Lacy. I'm too scared to tell you any more. Too scared of you.

Well, you didn't look all that scared last night! he laughed. My! That was some blow you landed on me.

Jasmin was shivering. Downstairs the boys were playing music on the PA system that they'd rigged up for the party. Jasmin tried to clear her head, struggled to stay calm.

What were you doing at the party? she asked him.

Do you mean was I invited? Well, yes I was actually. I happened to be in the pub last evening, and I got the word from one of the boys who lives in your house there.

And he told you to bring your wife, too, did he?

My *wife*! Why do you keep asking me about my wife? Who said I was married in the first place?

Well, girlfriend then. Whatever.

Lacy sighed. The lady last night was my landlady. Her name's Carol. Her husband was there in the room with us when you blew in. Would you like me to fetch her, so that she can verify my statements? Or would you prefer something in writing?

Stop it, Lacy, said Jasmin angrily. You've got no right to mock me.

Everyone's got a right to mock everyone else, he answered breezily. You take yourself much too seriously, princess. And then you try to make other people take you seriously too. It does you no good. Not in the long run.

You're a bastard, Lacy. A real bastard. (But there was no malice in what she was saying. There was no point in Jasmin trying to hurt Lacy. She knew it was beyond her capabilities. And besides, she wanted him too much. She still wanted him too much.) So you say you're not married then?

Cross my heart.

And what about your kids? The ones you tell bedtime stories to?

160

Lacy laughed. They're not *my* kids, love! You've got it all wrong. They're Carol's boys, my landlady's. I call them my boys, that's all. They're not my flesh and blood, like. Is that okay now?

Jasmin wanted to believe him. Desperately she wanted to believe him. But there was so much against it being true. So much.

And the girl in the canal that day? she asked. Who was she?

I really don't know what you're talking about there, he laughed. I didn't understand you the other day. I was on my own. There wasn't any girl.

I don't believe you, Jasmin said dejectedly. You don't say things that sound real. Sometimes I think you're not even real yourself. I think I must have . . . conjured you up out of nothing. Conjured you up just to plague me. Me and my wreck of a family.

He didn't reply to that. Jasmin had said it almost without thinking. But in the pause that followed she wondered if she might have strayed too close to the truth. But how could she have conjured him up, and from where? Saddened, and frightened, she could scarcely believe that these were her own thoughts.

You're wearing me down, Lacy, she said quickly. Why the hell were you taking photos outside my house last week?

Photos?

There was a long, thick silence. To make any sense of all this, Jasmin had to see his face, his eyes. She had to be able to touch him. She had to be intoxicated by that strange plastery smell of his skin. The truth was inside him. It wasn't available to her over the telephone.

Lacy, she said, screwing up her face, Can we meet?

I think that would probably be the best idea, he replied, mimicking the gravity in her voice.

This afternoon?

Ah, now that would be tricky. How about dinner on Friday night?

Jasmin rolled her eyes. Friday was four days away. Four days might be longer than she could wait. Can't you make it any earlier? We don't have to have dinner.

Oh, I think we do, he laughed. That's usually the way these things are done, love, isn't it?

What did he mean? Jasmin was almost certain that he was referring obliquely to Roland, to her and Roland. He knew it all, everything.

I'll call for you about seven then, on Friday, all right? Oh, and by the way, I think someone at the party must have knocked your little dragon into the bin. You know, the dragon I gave you in St. David's? I put it up on your stereo. Out of harm's way, like.

Thank you, Lacy, said Jasmin. That was very thoughtful.

That's right, he said. You don't want to lose it now. It'll bring you luck, you see.

Luck, thought Jasmin when she'd put the phone down. She took the clay dragon down from its place on her music center. How had Lacy known that she'd kept it there before throwing it away?

She inspected it all over. She held it to her ear and shook it. *Don't go giving it away now,* Lacy had said in St. David's. For a few moments, she had an absurd idea that the dragon had been bugged. That Lacy was monitoring her every sigh and shiver.

I'm still here, Lacy, she said loudly into the dragon's

cross-eyed face. I know you're there, I wish you'd leave me alone . . . I wish, oh, God, I wish I wish, I wish, I wish . . .

And then she chuckled despondently, put the dragon back, and began to wait for Friday.

27

IT WAS A LONG AND TAXING WAIT.

What was it that Lacy had said? *In the day of trouble I shall be of more use to you than three hundred salmon.* Jasmin was annoyed that his verbiage had lodged itself so firmly in her head. But was Friday going to be the day? Did Lacy somehow know in advance? And how, exactly, was he going to be of *use* to her? (She took it for granted that Lacy knew the answers to these questions. She really took it for granted that he knew more about her than she knew about herself.)

She didn't ring Roland. Roland rang her though, twice. They both steered clear of any intimate talk, but during their second conversation Jasmin suddenly burst into tears. It was just the sound of his voice. So restful, so understanding. And Jasmin had made love with him without her diaphragm . . . But she had no intention of telling him about that, neither him nor anyone else.

I'm so sorry, she sobbed to him, So very sorry. I'm . . . I'm finding it quite hard to handle things at the moment. It won't last though. I'll be all right soon.

Every day Jasmin spoke briefly with Eileen. Until that Wednesday, her mother continued to sound buoyant. She seemed to be getting along famously with Kate, she was happy with Sidney's progress. And Michael had made a lightning visit to the house from Brussels, confirming that his closest family would be delighted to come to Eileen's party.

Then on Wednesday morning Sidney left the hospital. He refused point blank to return home while Kate was still there. (He'd stopped her from visiting him at the hospital too.) Kate offered immediately to go back to Belgium. But Eileen wouldn't hear of it. So Sidney went to stay with old Frank.

I wanted Kate here, Eileen told Jasmin later on the phone. (She made it sound so cut and dried.)

But it's Sidney's home, said Jasmin. He shouldn't be kept out of his own home.

No one's keeping him out. It's his choice entirely. We'd love to have him here. But if he chooses to bear this grudge, well, that's his affair. We can't all keep living in the past. I can't, anyway.

Jasmin said nothing.

It's all right, Jas. I go up and see him regularly. And he's got old Frank's nurse to look after him too. Don't worry so. He's quite all right, really he is.

Are you sure? asked Jasmin.

Positive.

But afterwards she became even more uneasy. She couldn't help sensing that there was something else, something that Eileen hadn't got around to telling her. It played on Jasmin's mind. At one especially fraught stage, she even considered that Sidney might have died, and that Eileen was planning to break the truth to her in installments.

She knew that she was bearing up badly under all the strain. It was beginning to show in her appearance. Around the eyes, around the mouth, in the slow way that she moved about her room. Lawrence, her agent, noticed this when he called in for a chat on Thursday morning.

He'd obviously come to see whether she'd read Roland's story. But when he saw how she was looking he said nothing about work at all. The look of her seemed to upset him. Politely he suggested that she should see a doctor. Jasmin pooh-poohed the idea. She said that her sabbatical season wouldn't be lasting much longer. Then she'd be getting down to Roland's story. She promised.

Behind the business talk, she found it rather amusing that Lawrence didn't know about her and Roland. As far as Lawrence was concerned, Roland was just the author of a story which Jasmin wouldn't read. Nothing more.

It suited Jasmin to keep it like that. It was none of Lawrence's business. It was nobody's business but her own. And anyway, she couldn't expect Roland to put up with her indefinitely. She couldn't expect his patience to hold much longer. Perhaps he'd even decided to throw in the towel already? It was several days since he'd been in touch.

But there was nothing for Jasmin to do except wait. She just sat at the window, watching the woman and the girl in the next garden, and sometimes the old man, too.

She knew that she ought to be occupying herself with work. But she couldn't bear the thought of it. Not even reading poor Roland's story. She'd been away from her work for far longer than she'd originally thought possible. She was beginning to run very short of cash. But even that didn't tempt her to shift herself.

I've stopped wanting to work, she thought, intrigued rather than demoralized. This break hasn't rekindled my enthusiasm for work at all. It's killed it, stone dead. But Kate just stopped working. Why can't I do the same? Why can't I be like Kate? *Why?* . . .

And then on Friday, as if to rub salt into the wound, all her working materials were dumped back in her room. The fourth boy had decided to return from southern Europe a couple of weeks early. Naturally, he wanted his room back. So Jasmin was once again hemmed in by her easels, her portfolios, her worktop, her stool. Ranged around her, they were, like accusations. Accusations which she couldn't begin to answer.

I've got to get out, she thought. I've got to get out of this place and I've got to get out of the twilight. I do need you now, Lacy, I do. Get me out. I don't care how you do it. Just get me out.

And Lacy arrived, just as he'd promised, at seven o'clock.

28

Lacy didn't take her to a restaurant. It was a pub in the country, some ten miles outside the city, on the road to Jasmin's home town.

Lacy drove them in a black Opel Manta, which he handled with great expertise. She didn't ask him where the car had come from. That kind of question no longer seemed so urgent. (This was the first time that she'd been alone with him since coming back from Wales. It was vitally important for her to make every word count.)

He seemed to be his old ebullient self on the journey, talking as enthusiastically as ever, about snooker, birds, car rallying, discos. Jasmin was convinced that he kept saying

the first thing that came into his head. But, as she had discovered on that very first Saturday, it was easy to enjoy the
rhythms of his speech without taking serious note of the
content. He spoke at a leisurely pace. He didn't require
many answers or comments. He made Jasmin feel like a
child, or a parent—someone, at any rate, who couldn't be
considered an equal.

Is your father improving? he asked as they entered the
pub.

In a way, said Jasmin. She felt as if she was walking on
the thinnest sheet of ice.

How do you mean—in a way?

I'm not sure. I . . . I don't think my mother is telling
me everything I should know. Please don't let's talk about
it, Lacy. Please.

She sat on a bench opposite Lacy and studied the menu.
Burgers, pizza, club sandwiches, chili. Most of the other
customers were bikers. She felt conspicuous in her black
backless dress, her white crocheted shawl. She wished she
hadn't bothered with makeup and jewelry. But how could
she have known that Lacy was going to bring her here?
How could she have known?

She had no appetite. Lacy told her that the chili was
usually good, so she ordered some. The jukebox music pre-
vented them from talking while they waited for the food.
They sipped their drinks and looked at each other.

Lacy was wearing a beret. A beret, a brown leather
bomber jacket, and a pair of baggy black trousers which
narrowed sharply towards the ankle.

Every time Jasmin had seen Lacy in twentieth-century
dress he'd concealed himself in brand-new clothes. (Every
time, that was, except at that encounter by the canal.) Nothing about his clothes gave any clue to his personality, po-

sition or origin. It was as if he was dressing to commit a crime.

Jasmin looked at him and she wanted him so badly. He seemed strong to her that night. Powerfully built, gentle in his gestures. He had his elbows on the table, his soft hands pressed together in a praying position in front of his lips. He's as real as I am, thought Jasmin. I haven't conjured him from anywhere. And he has to be the man. He has to be.

The food arrived. Earthenware bowls of chili con carne which hadn't been properly reheated. Jasmin couldn't be bothered to complain. She ate a few mouthfuls, out of politeness. Lacy urged her to eat more. You look as if you haven't eaten for weeks, he told her. But she noticed that Lacy barely touched his own.

It didn't make sense, Lacy bringing her here. He had a taste for good food, she'd seen that in St. David's. So what was he trying to prove by this? She noticed that he was becoming withdrawn. He was going unusually easy on the beer, too. Then quite suddenly he said that they should be getting away.

She allowed him to pay the bill. (She hadn't forgotten that they still hadn't settled up for the weekend in Wales. But it was going to be harder for her to pay her share now. She was running out of money fast.) The daylight hadn't quite faded when they left the pub and made for the car park. Now, thought Jasmin. It's got to be now . . .

They came to the car. Jasmin took Lacy's arm and tried to turn him toward her. He stiffened, but wheeled around. He was looking over her head, running his tongue over his top lip. A snatch of jukebox music lapped toward them from the pub, then melted into the air.

Jasmin pushed her hands inside his jacket and rested her palms flat against his chest. He was wearing a subtle after-shave, but she could still make out that dusty, plastery smell of his skin.

Lacy, she said quietly, looking at his throat, Lacy . . .

He wouldn't yield. He gripped her shoulders and tried to hold her away from him. His hands were cold through her crocheted shawl. She pressed herself back into him. She looked up into his face.

And all at once the fight went out of her. Her head went down, she let her shoulders droop. She just couldn't do this any more. His eyes had somehow gouged away her sense of purpose. If Lacy had suddenly let her go, she might well have fallen to the muddy ground in a heap. Some bikers had come out of the pub, spotted Jasmin and Lacy, and began to whistle through their teeth.

Come on, love, said Lacy. He led her to the passenger door. Jasmin got into the car as if she were being worked by remote control. Lacy pulled off his jacket, threw it into the back and climbed into the driver's seat.

He pointed out a bag of pears at her feet, and another bag, full of shelled hazel nuts. But Jasmin wasn't hearing him. She was thinking in her disembodied way: He'll drive me home, I'll get out of the car, I'll go back to my room, I'll drink something, I'll probably cry, I'll struggle to get to sleep, I won't be too keen to wake up . . .

I'm sick of my life, she thought, as Lacy drove out into the country lanes. And I'm losing the will to want to change it.

Lacy said nothing. He turned on the car radio. He played with the dial until he came to a station playing rock music. Then he wound down the window and rested his elbow half in and half out of the car. He looked as if he was setting himself up for a long drive.

It was only then that Jasmin realized that he had joined a main road, and was driving away from the city.

What! . . . she cried, rocking herself forward in her seat. What are you doing? Where are we going? Lacy, where are we going?

He arched his neck and looked at her over his cheekbone. He was driving the Manta outrageously fast. There's no need to panic now, is there? he said.

Where the hell are you taking me? Jasmin shouted, throwing herself from side to side in her seat, watching all the wrong landmarks flying past. Stop or I'll scream!

Stop or I'll scream? Lacy repeated with a genuine laugh. *Stop or I'll scream?* Well, what do you know! And there was me thinking women had stopped saying things like that!

Jasmin closed her eyes, tight. Please Lacy, she murmured. Why are you doing this to me? Please, please tell me where we're going.

Where do you think? Back home of course. To see your mum and your dad. You said you were worried about your dad. You thought your mum wasn't telling you something. Well I think it's best that you go and find out, don't you?

Jasmin began to tingle from her shoulders slowly downwards. *In the day of trouble . . .* Deep inside herself she'd known from the start that this was going to happen, that it had to happen. Now it was happening. And there wasn't a thing she could do about it.

She looked at Lacy. He seemed so big and bluff and innocuous. Perhaps, in spite of everything, that's all he was. Big and bluff and innocuous. Someone who wasn't too keen on sex. Someone who simply wanted to put her mind at rest, to stop her from making herself more unhappy than she needed to be. It was possible. Despite everything, it was possible. Jasmin prayed that it was true.

172

Is . . . is anyone going to get hurt? she asked timidly after several minutes had passed.

What questions you ask, princess! How can I say? I'm just the driver. You'll have to give me directions, mind, once we get to the town. I'd say we could be there in under the hour.

I'm going to get hurt, thought Jasmin, staring through her reflection in the side window. It's going to be me. And he knows . . .

29

THE LIGHTS WERE OUT IN THE DOWNSTAIRS ROOMS. KATE WAS in the bath and Eileen was in bed. It was some time before Eileen got down to open the front door. When she saw Jasmin and Lacy standing there, she looked as if she'd seen the risen Christ. Lacy took off his beret.

Eileen didn't say much. She just led them into the kitchen, poured some glasses of vodka, and beamed at the two of them in deep delight. Jasmin coughed, and began to fabricate a reason for their visit. Almost at once she gave up. Eileen didn't care why they had come. They were there. That was all that mattered to her.

Jasmin's told you, I expect, she said to Lacy, That I've dreamed about you.

Is that so? said Lacy, grinning. He looked vast in that crowded kitchen. A big mellow bear on his best behavior. He drank his vodka and gladly accepted another. Jasmin leaned against the kitchen wall and kept quiet. It was as if she'd been bringing Lacy home all her life. She was the third person out of three in there. Something was going to happen. She knew that. But it was going to happen to her, not because of her.

Eileen was telling Lacy about the preparations for the party. She was inviting him to come. She was filling him in on the details of Kate's marriage, Sidney's stroke. Lacy just nodded, the big bear, the man who read photographs. Bluff, innocuous. He seemed to be enjoying himself immensely. Jasmin had never known him to stay silent for so long.

And as for the carving, Eileen said eventually, Well, I won't say anything now because I've written you a thank-you note. I was going to send it to Jasmin. To pass on to you. But now that you're here, I'll be able to give it to you in person. (She winked at him. *Winked!* Jasmin had no words to frame what she felt. No words at all.)

There was a stirring behind the kitchen door and Kate came into the room. Hot-faced from the bath, she'd thrown one of Eileen's old dressing gowns over her baggy pajamas. She looked exquisite. She smiled at Jasmin. Not a knowing smile or the smile of a rival. Just a smile.

Lacy got to his feet to be introduced. He clicked his heels and gave his little bow. Jasmin remembered that once he'd done the same for her. Kate smiled and ran a hand, slowly, through her damp hair.

175

Lacy and Kate, together. Jasmin had been imagining this meeting. Not just on that night in St. David's, when she'd been lying in bed and staring at the photo. Not just then. It went back much further. Jasmin felt as if she'd been imagining this meeting ever since she'd had an imagination to misuse.

No one seemed to know what to say next. Eileen clearly felt that words were superfluous. Lacy looked at his feet. And in the end it was Kate who spoke up.

Now that she's here, you've got to tell her, she said to Eileen.

Eileen drew her dressing gown tighter around her. Oh, she said. It can wait. You won't be going back until the morning now, will you, Jas?

Kate ran her hand through her hair again. Please, mum, she said. She has a right to know.

A right to know what? cried Jasmin, pushing herself off the wall. What are you talking about for God's sake? (But through her head a single word was pulsing—Sidney, Sidney, Sidney . . .)

Eileen reached out, across the kitchen counter, and laid her hand on Jasmin's. It's your father, she said comfortingly. He's going to go back to Warsaw.

The kitchen at that moment seemed extraordinarily bright to Jasmin. Going back for good? she asked, but already she knew what Eileen's answer would be.

Eileen duly nodded. She was smiling. There were no tears in her eyes.

He's going back without you? (Jasmin was automatically delivering lines from a play she'd scripted for herself more than twenty years before.)

My place isn't there, Jas. You know that.

Kate had turned her lovely face to the kitchen door. Lacy

176

unscrewed the top of the bottle of vodka and poured Jasmin a large measure. She drank it. She hardly felt it slipping down inside her. *So it takes something out of the ordinary to bring you all together, then?*

Jasmin stared from Eileen to Lacy. For reasons that would have been unclear to anyone but Jasmin, she wanted to hit Lacy. But she'd already done that. She'd already done that . . .

Eileen leaned forward and squeezed Jasmin's hand hard. Jasmin was still staring at Lacy. His face was heavy with commiseration. He shrugged. His vodka glass looked minuscule in his hand.

Look, he said to Eileen, I'll go into the other room. You'll be wanting to talk. I'll go.

Jasmin watched him walk out of the kitchen, past Kate.

Go with him, Kate, said Eileen. I'll stay and talk to Jas. Give him another drink. Look after him.

Kate left the kitchen too. To look after Lacy.

Jasmin's eyes were following the patterns on the roll of kitchen paper in front of her. That's what I'll do, she was thinking. It's what I've got to do. I'll come back here and live with Eileen. Just the two of us. That's the way it has to be now . . .

I told Sidney, Eileen was saying, I told him that he mustn't stay here just on my account. It's been coming for years, this. I've always been prepared for it. I suppose we all have. It . . . it hasn't done anything to me, Jasmin. That's the God's honest truth.

Jasmin felt faint. Lacy's voice and then Kate's voice wafted in from the front room. Serious murmured conversation, profound silences. She wanted Lacy with her. With her, being of use, in the day of trouble. Not with Kate, not out of her sight.

She looked into Eileen's eyes. She knew all her lines. She knew exactly what she had to say. *I'll come back here. I'll live with you here. Just the two of us . . .* But she couldn't open her mouth. She closed her eyes, then opened them, hoping that the words would somehow have said themselves in the meantime. They hadn't.

Come back in here, Lacy, she thought. Don't be away from me. Don't be with Kate. Don't be with Kate. She's got too much. Even without you she's got too much . . .

What on earth, she said to her mother at last. What on earth are you going to do?

It's all taken care of, Eileen replied, pressing the palms of her hands flat against the kitchen counter. I'm going to move in with Kate and Michael.

Jasmin looked at her in despair. Kate and Michael? she said. You can't be serious? You won't go to Poland but you'll live with Kate in Brussels?

Eileen clasped her hands together and flexed her fingers. (My mother's no longer a sane person, thought Jasmin. And, realizing this, she felt more hopeless than she'd felt at any time during that whole disastrous summer.) Yes, Jasmin, I will go with Kate. If I find it strange at first, I'll just make myself enjoy it. I want it to work. I want to make a bit of a break for myself, you know, before it's too late. And there's something else, too . . .

Yes? . . . Go on. I can't imagine what else there could be.

Well, she lowered her voice and smiled, Kate didn't want me to tell you this, not yet. But, yes, you were right, all of us were right. She *is* pregnant. She's expecting in January. Jasmin, I'm going to be a granny!

Jasmin could only make a disparaging noise through her nose and mouth. A depressed noise. A noise of envy and bitterness. So Kate wants you over there to look after the baby for her, is that it?

Eileen reached out and patted Jasmin's hand. When you've had children of your own, she said, you'll understand. But you're upset now. A lot of things have been happening. When the dust has settled you'll see that it's been for the best. All of this. You will, Jas. It's a kind of shake-up. This family's been needing a shake-up for so long. And we're going to be all right. I know that. I know that from my dream.

Jasmin stepped down from the stool. She rubbed her hand across the side of her face. Your dream! she said with great sadness. Your dream! And how do you think I'm going to be all right? What's going to happen to me?

Eileen looked her full in the face. You've got Roland, she said simply.

Roland? *Roland?* What's he got to do with it? I thought it was Lacy you were mad keen on.

Eileen shook her head. Lacy is different, Jas. He's something special, something out of the ordinary. I knew that even before I met him here. But I don't think he's right, for you. Not the way Roland's right for you. Do you know what I mean? Jas, it's going to work out. Trust me.

Jasmin walked slowly to the kitchen door. My mother's not all there, she thought, then stopped herself from thinking any more. But she knew what she was going to do. She knew what she had to do. Lacy and Kate stopped talking and looked up as she entered the front room. Eileen followed her in. It was late. Time to sort out the sleeping arrangements and turn in.

But Jasmin knew what she had to do.

30

JASMIN LAY IN HER UNDERWEAR ON THE COUNTERPANE OF HER bed. Her bed. Her room. This was where she'd grown up worried. Beside this bed she'd begged God to send Sidney back from Poland. There was still one of her old pictures on the wall. A psychedelic poster for a concert by the group Kevin Ayers and the Whole World.

This, then, was the final reckoning. This was how the giant was going to set them all down again. Sidney would at last get his discharge—and a basically honorable one, too. Eileen would slip into the bosom of her new young family. Kate would have her rich husband—and plenty of time on her hands if she felt like keeping up with a few other men as well, as Kate most surely would. Old Alice was in a far, far better place. And then there was Jasmin. Then there was Jasmin and what *she* wanted.

The night around her coaxed gentle murmurs from the windowpane and fireplace. In the next room, her parents' room, Eileen and Kate were sleeping in the twin beds. Jasmin had listened to them whispering to each other, giggling intermittently, then finally falling silent.

The pale moonlight coated the end of Jasmin's bed and the stack of empty suitcases beyond it. Soon the suitcases would be full. This house was going to be abandoned. Just as Jasmin was going to be abandoned. And down the landing, in the third and smallest bedroom, was what *Jasmin* wanted.

She got to her feet, undid her bra and slipped out of her panties. There's nowhere else to go after this, she thought. This is as far as I can go.

Her body was clamoring for Lacy, racing on ahead of her and bursting into his room. Naked she stepped out onto the landing. She could hear Eileen snoring. Lacy's door was slightly ajar. A dull light showed beneath it and in the narrow space along its side.

The landing wasn't long. She approached the door on tiptoe. The door of what used to be Kate's room. He was in there, the big bear, cornered. Even if he didn't want her, he was going to get her. He'd led her this far. He'd led them all this far. But now, once again, the initiative had to fall to Jasmin.

She stopped at the door and inclined her head. There was a scraping sound inside, as if he was sharpening a pencil. She didn't knock. She didn't scratch a warning.

She slipped into his room and closed the door behind her.

Lacy was sitting, fully clothed, on the edge of the bed. By the light of the bedside lamp he was working with a knife at a piece of white wood. He'd spread a magazine on the carpet to catch the shavings.

He didn't look up at once. With great deliberation he slid the piece of wood into his trouser pocket. It was as if he'd wanted Jasmin to *see* what he'd been carving. It looked like a gargoyle, a tiny gargoyle. She leaned back against the door, her arms stiff at her sides.

Slowly Lacy raised his face. The unsheathed knife glinted in his hand. Jasmin could see no eyes at all. Just the shadows, just the shadows. He ran his tongue over his top lip. He looked far too big for that room. Far too big, far too unlikely. He looked surprised to see her. Nothing more.

Put the knife away, Jasmin whispered.

Lacy glanced down. He pressed his forefinger lightly against the tip of the blade. You've come through the wrong door, he said, without looking up. That wasn't a door you should have come through, my love.

Jasmin shuddered. She felt awesomely cold. Hold me, Lacy, she said. Hold me, please . . .

Lacy, still sitting, laid the knife beside the base of the lamp. As soon as it was out of his hand, she threw herself forward. Her face was buried in his shoulder. Her legs were astride one of his thighs. The plaster smell of his neck. The day's growth of his beard. He'd fallen back so that his shoulders were against the wall.

Jasmin kissed his throat, his collarbone. She reached down, beneath his waist. He was talking. Urgent whispers. He was saying no. He was saying, No my love. Not like this . . .

Jasmin floundered on. She reached up and kissed him

on the mouth. She was gripping his arms and kissing him on the cheek. She kissed him hard between his eyes.

Lacy was attempting to shake his head away. Jasmin tried to wheel him on top of her. She'd never regarded herself as a demonstrative lovemaker. Now she was surging deeper and deeper into foreign, increasingly hostile territory. Then Lacy grabbed her two-handed by her waist, lifted her bodily on to the duvet beside him, and pinned her down.

Jasmin squinted at his eyes. Shadows, all shadows. Or was it, now that she fought her way up closer to him, was it *more* than that? Was there instead some faint flush about his head that was throwing the recesses of his face into shadow? Was it—oh, God, was it?—a kind of *incandescence*? . . .

A genuine *glow*?

He was breathing fast. His hands were pressed hard against her shoulders. For one awful moment she thought he was going to reach behind him for his knife. Instead he clapped a hand to the top of his head. Such a large, bald head. Such a small face on such a large bald head. Jasmin tried to tell herself that his pate was simply reflecting the lamplight. He's ugly, she thought. He's really ugly.

Why won't you make love to me? gasped Jasmin. She knew that they must have woken Kate and Eileen.

Love? he repeated. He looked so fierce. Love? (He said it in such a way that he managed to deprive the word of all its power and texture.)

Why Lacy? Jasmin asked again. Her body had gone limp beneath him. She could smell him. She'd have given her life to have him. She knew that if she didn't have him, her life would never be her own again.

He smiled. Not an amused smile. The smile of someone

who has nothing better to do with his face. The radiance had gone from him. You came through the wrong door, he told her softly. You're doing this the wrong way. It's not like that, love. *I'm* not like that.

So just what are you like, Lacy? Jasmin hissed up at him. Tell me that. What are you?

He looked away. He didn't exactly look at a loss. But he said nothing.

I don't think you're *real*, Jasmin went on. I don't think you're flesh and blood. There's nothing inside you. Nothing real. Nothing I can understand. You're no one, Lacy. No one at all. I've summoned you up from some unthinkable place and I wish to hell you'd get back there now and leave us all alone!

I don't think you mean that, he said, letting her go, then standing over her. You're a beautiful woman, he told her. There's nothing wrong with the way you look. You must believe me.

He's got no guts, thought Jasmin, dragging back the duvet and climbing into Lacy's bed. I've been right all along. He's scared of it. He's scared of himself . . .

Sharp pains had started to shoot through her abdomen. You can either sleep with me here, she said as proudly as she could, or else you can sleep on your own in my room. I'm not moving now.

And Lacy went.

Carefully he gathered up his knife and his watch and his magazine full of shavings. Jasmin watched him with contempt—a man who was nothing. He left the room. Then he came back moments later with the pile of Jasmin's discarded clothes. He didn't say a word.

When he was gone, truly gone, Jasmin began to tremble as she'd never trembled before. The pains in her abdomen stabbed sharper still, then fell away. She left the lamp on and closed her eyes. The smell of him was still with her. That was all. It was impossible for her to grasp how much she'd lost in a single evening. She curled up under the duvet, too traumatized to cry.

Sooner than she'd have dared to hope, she drifted off to sleep. She dreamed and she dreamed until at last she found herself back in the palace, back in the grip of the song. She was in front of the middle door, deep in the darkness. She reached for the handle, but she couldn't bring herself to turn it. The singing was lifting her up, away. The wrong door. It's the wrong door, Lacy was telling her. Trust me. It's going to be all right . . .

She woke up slowly, as if she were rising to the surface of a deep, still lake. She was sobbing. Outside her window there was birdsong. It's all right, said a voice. It's going to be all right. Jasmin could feel a hand clasped over her own.

She opened her eyes. Eileen was sitting on the bed beside her, dressed in her day clothes.

Poor Jas, she said, stroking Jasmin's hair. Why were you sobbing? What was it, love?

Jasmin closed her eyes again. It was good to feel her mother's hand on her hair. It was nothing, she said quietly. It wasn't anything. Really.

31

JASMIN WAS THE LAST TO COME DOWN FOR BREAKFAST. SHE wondered whether anyone was going to mention the fracas in the night, the fact that she and Lacy had swapped bedrooms. She'd expected Lacy to be gone. But there he was, as large as life at the kitchen counter, chatting to Eileen and Kate about mortgages.

He stood and gave Jasmin his stool. He was wearing the beret but he hadn't shaved. Already his stubble looked thick, protective. She drank some coffee but couldn't eat a thing. Her head felt thunderous. The pains in her stomach had come back and were turning into cramps.

Lacy's carving stood before her on the windowsill. The

186

carving in which Sidney didn't figure. Jasmin shielded her eyes, and drank some more coffee.

Eileen, with stunning insensitivity, was suggesting that Kate should go back to the city with Jasmin and Lacy. You could stay with Jas for a day or two, she said. It would be a nice break for you, Kate. You must be getting bored, stuck here with me all the time.

But Kate, to Jasmin's undisguised relief, wasn't interested. Jasmin looked across at Lacy. Did he look disappointed? Or was she imagining it? Did it even matter any more? (Jasmin knew that the last question was disingenuous. *Of course* it still mattered. Inside her, everything was just the same.)

Eileen turned to Jasmin. You'll call and see your father, won't you? she said. On your way home? He'll be wanting to see you.

Jasmin shrugged. Yes. Yes. (Then she looked scathingly at Lacy.) Unless you're in a desperate rush to get back?

Oh, no, he said. No rush, my love. We were talking about it before you came down, you see. Kate's going to come with us to your uncle's place . . .

You can talk to Sidney, Jas, Eileen said quickly. He'll listen to you. Try to get him to see Kate. I can't persuade him. He won't take any notice of what I say. You'll try, won't you?

Jasmin looked, in some bewilderment, at the three of them. Whatever became of my own free will? she thought. But she nodded her head, because there was really nothing else that she could do.

Eileen followed them out to the car. She handed Lacy her thank you note for the carving, and reminded him to be sure to come to the party. He read the note on the spot, smiled, and crammed it into his back pocket. It was a sharp, wintry morning. It made Jasmin feel more hemmed in than ever.

Are you all right, love? Eileen asked. Why are you holding your stomach?

It's nothing, said Jasmin, wincing. A few pains . . .

Is it something you've eaten?

And Jasmin swayed imperceptibly as she remembered that bowl of lukewarm chili at the bikers' pub. The chili that Lacy had been so keen for her to eat. The chili that Lacy himself had only picked at.

No, said Jasmin. It's nothing, nothing . . .

In the car she began to feel slightly better. Kate was sitting in the front seat beside Lacy. Pregnant Kate. Jasmin watched her handing him hazel nuts. She said nothing. She left all the talking to Lacy. Talking was what he was good at.

Then, quite out of the blue, he began to describe to the two of them a nightclub up north. At the end of the description, he claimed that the nightclub owner, a friend of his, had asked him to manage the place for a couple of months. Jasmin raised her eyebrows. She didn't believe a word of it.

So you're moving on then, Lacy? she asked him sarcastically.

Oh, I might, he said over his shoulder. I don't know yet.

It doesn't do to fester, does it? said Jasmin.

No, love, he laughed. It certainly doesn't. And a change is as good as a rest, they say.

Lacy and Kate stayed in the car while Jasmin knocked at old Frank's door. The nurse answered, a dumpy, cheerful woman holding a dustpan and brush. She gave Jasmin a peculiar look. Jasmin couldn't blame her. She was still wearing her cocktail dress and shawl. She probably looked as if she was on her way home from a night on the town.

The nurse led the way through to the middle room. Old Frank was in his usual chair. He smiled at her. Sidney was sitting on the other side of the fireplace. He looked fit, and not in the least surprised to see her. Jasmin sat at the table, while the nurse continued to clean around her. She chatted briefly with old Frank, hovering around the subject of Alice but never daring to mention her name. This wasn't the right place to say what she wanted to say to her father. It couldn't have been more wrong.

Can we go into the garden? she finally asked Sidney.

He led the way out on to old Frank's bit of lawn. They stood virtually side by side, only inches away from where they'd posed for old Frank's photo. That photo. So long ago now. The photo that bore so much responsibility.

Mum told me, said Jasmin quickly, falteringly, about you . . .

It was cold in the fresh air. The nurse had told her not to keep him out there for too long.

Sidney lit a cigarette. He nodded, exhaled the smoke towards his feet. He was wearing a pair of old Frank's slippers.

I'm sorry, Dad, she said. I'm sorry you're going. I . . .

The words caught in her throat and she began to cry. Sidney threw away his cigarette. He turned her to face him, drew her to him. He put his arms around her and she cried powerfully into his shoulder, repeating a single all-encompassing word over and over: Dad, Dad, Dad, Dad . . .

Sidney caressed her back until her body stopped heaving, then he offered her his handkerchief. She blew her nose, but almost doubled up in pain as another of the spasms racked her stomach.

189

I'm all right, she told Sidney. I'll be all right.

You've got someone, haven't you? said her father. That boy you brought—Roland? He likes you. He said to me, he's very fond of you.

Jasmin nodded her head. Yes, she whispered. I know . . . I've got someone.

Perhaps you should settle down as well? You could take a longer break from your work then. If you wanted to. I know, Jasmin, I know it hasn't been . . . easy. You should be happier. You mustn't be like this.

Yes, Jasmin said again. I'm sorry . . .

The nurse tapped on the kitchen window and waved them in. Jasmin took Sidney's hand as they stepped over the tiny rock garden. Will you see Kate? she asked. She's outside. In the car.

No, said Sidney, raising his eyebrows. (His voice betrayed nothing of what he thought, but it was a voice with which Jasmin couldn't even think of arguing.) No . . .

Jasmin looked at him. They were as close to each other as they had ever been—and still as far apart. There wasn't any other way for them to be. She kissed his cheek, said goodbye to old Frank, and opened the front door. Sidney closed it, quickly, as soon as she was outside.

Kate was standing on the pavement, leaning against the car. Lacy was standing beside her. They'd had plenty of time to do their talking.

Jasmin shook her head at them and shrugged.

Shall *I* have a word with him? asked Lacy.

You! said Jasmin derisively, before shaking her head with more vigor than before.

They said their goodbyes where they stood. Kate then walked to the bottom of the street to wait for a bus back to Eileen's house. Pregnant Kate. Married and pregnant, sorted out.

See you, Lacy had said after shaking her by the hand. See you.

Twice in the next half hour Lacy asked Jasmin if she wanted him to pull over. You really don't look very bright, he said.

Isn't this how you want me to look? thought Jasmin, seeing the bowl of chili again. She clutched at her stomach and told him to drive on. She couldn't have said anything more to him now. With Sidney, with Lacy—the two men she was losing—she'd run right out of words. She gazed grimly out of her side window. Even the cars they were passing looked cold.

By the time they reached the city the spasms had become almost continuous. She felt dreadfully carsick too. She felt sure that if she were to move her head just a fraction, she would begin to vomit uncontrollably. Again Lacy asked if he should stop. Again Jasmin growled at him to get her home.

When they reached her house it was raining. Lacy opened Jasmin's door for her, and made as if to help her indoors. Feebly she tried to slap his hands away. But Lacy took hold of her anyway. And she was glad.

The little girl from the next-door garden was out on the pavement, astride her bicycle.

What's the matter with the lady? she asked Lacy.

She's not very well, my love, Lacy told her. Nothing to worry about, though. She'll be as right as ninepence in a bit.

Lacy humped her around to the kitchen door. Once she was indoors, she was able to do without his help, staggering from one piece of furniture to another like a baby finding its feet. Nonetheless, she was sorry when he let her go.

She propped herself against the doorway to the hall. Someone was playing an acoustic guitar in the lounge. She sensed that Lacy was no longer right behind her. She looked over her shoulder.

He was standing by the kitchen door, running a hand across his unshaven cheek, looking as if he were on the point of leaving. One of the cats had keeled over at his feet and was rubbing its head against his shoe.

You can't go, pleaded Jasmin. You *can't* go now! I need you. You can't go.

It's not me that you need, princess, he said with a radiant smile, Not yet.

And he rapped twice on the kitchen door with his knuckles, then left the house.

32

AFTERWARD, JASMIN COULDN'T REMEMBER EXACTLY HOW SHE
made it from the kitchen doorway to her room. She remembered the vicious spasm of pain that all but prostrated
her when Lacy slammed the door. Then there was only the
sight of her bed, coming up to claim her as she toppled
over.

When Roland entered the room he found her curled up
in a ball, completely cocooned in her duvet. She was breathing in short shallow bursts, her face clammy, her hair matted
and tangled.

As soon as he took her by the shoulders she threw up
for the first time. He got her into the bathroom before she

started to retch again. She was aware of him peeling off her sodden dress, wrapping her in a large towel. She knew, too, that the boys were there. *In the day of trouble . . .* she kept hearing. *In the day of trouble . . .* And she really couldn't tell whether she was saying the words herself or just listening to her memory.

The retching gave way to a second bout of vomiting. She felt as if someone had thrust a hand so far down her throat that it was tugging her bowels up into her chest. She cried out, once, twice.

Roland was holding her by her armpits. The bathroom sink swam in and out of her vision. Gasping, salivating, she begged Roland to get rid of the boys.

And then Roland was carrying her back to her room, swapping the soiled duvet for a clean one, easing her into her nightie. *In the day of trouble . . . In the day of trouble . . .* She put her arms and legs just where he told her. She was glad to concentrate on his instructions. Concentrating kept the giddiness at bay, kept the words away. You've had a bad bout, Roland was saying. A bad bout. But you'll be all right soon, soon . . .

By the time the doctor arrived, Jasmin was ready to start vomiting again. The doctor's face wasn't familiar. This is my doctor, Roland explained. He's a friend, too. I didn't know who your doctor was.

Jasmin listened semideliriously as Roland talked him through her previous twelve hours. How the hell did Roland know about all that? And why, now she came to think of it, had Roland made such a timely appearance at her house in the first place?

So your last meal was chili con carne? the doctor asked her.

194

Yes, she groaned, closing her eyes. Not hot. Not properly hot . . .

The doctor nodded. He injected her in the bottom, prescribed two sets of antibiotics, and left. Jasmin dragged herself back to the bathroom and tried to throw up again. She couldn't. There was nothing left inside her. She coughed and spat. She couldn't raise herself from her almost prone position.

Roland got her back under the duvet. Just a bad bout of food poisoning, he assured her. You'll start feeling better soon, once the injection takes.

Jasmin reached for his hand and pressed his palm against her temple. It felt wonderfully cool. His fingers stank of nicotine. She liked it. They stayed in that position for a very long time. Outside in the garden next door, the little girl was clattering up and down on her bicycle, singing unfamiliar songs at the top of her voice. Gradually Jasmin simmered down, and started to feel simply weary.

Back there, Roland said eventually, in the bathroom. You were saying something . . .

Jasmin snorted weakly and tried to smile. *In the day of trouble,* . . . she began.

I will be of greater service to thee than three hundred salmon, Roland concluded, looking highly amused.

Something like that, sighed Jasmin. You've heard it before?

Certainly I have, he chuckled, It's in that Taliesin book of mine. At least, my version of it is.

Oh, Christ, Jasmin said. Him again. I had a feeling it would be. The liberator of the lost . . .

I didn't know you'd read it.

I haven't, Jasmin told him wearily. I don't even know what it means. What does it mean?

It's just what Taliesin said, when this guy fished him out of a weir. The guy was there trying to catch salmon, you see . . .

And was he? Jasmin asked, thoughtful now. Taliesin? Helpful, I mean?

Oh, sure, said Roland, leaning over and kissing her on the forehead. Taliesin's always helpful. He's, well, he's a force for good. You know?

Jasmin waited for Roland to ask her why she'd been saying the words. She waited for him to ask her how she knew them. The little girl squealed on in the garden. But Roland said nothing.

Jasmin felt used up, too old for her own good, and perilously close to tears. She resettled her head on the pillow. (I don't know, she thought, It's all going away from me, everything . . .) Tell me, she said to Roland, Why did you come here? What made you come?

He smiled at her. It was your friend, he said. Lacy. He came to my place. I suppose he must have come as soon as he'd dropped you here.

That sounded wrong to Jasmin, drowsy as she was. It wouldn't lie down in her mind.

He said he had to go somewhere, he continued. But that you were under the weather, so could I get over and see to you? He told me what you'd been doing with him . . .

Jasmin let go of Roland's hand. She had begun to feel steadier now. Still drained, but steadier. The guitarist downstairs was playing again.

And you just came? said Jasmin, propping herself up on her elbow.

And I just came, said Roland with a smile. Do you mind if I have a fag?

Jasmin shook her head. How did he know where to find you?

Roland shrugged. He was rolling a cigarette. I don't know. I didn't stop to ask him. See, he made it sound pretty serious. I suppose he saw us together at the party. And he'd seen me down by the canal before. He must have put two and two together. Unless you gave him my address?

I gave him nothing, said Jasmin. (She paused. She was trying not to remember Lacy holding her down on the bed the night before. Lacy, and his ugly, shining head . . .) Didn't you think it was odd, she went on. I mean, Lacy coming to you? Not just calling a doctor?

Roland lit his cigarette. He shrugged. He just shrugged. Why wouldn't Roland see the oddness of Lacy? Why?

Jasmin thought hard before asking her next question. She guessed that she wasn't going to find much comfort in Roland's answer.

You don't mind then, that I was with Lacy last night?

Why should I mind? He stood, and peered out of the window.

Jasmin looked him up and down. He was a warm man, affectionate, willing, considerate. Why then was he so in-different when it came to Lacy? Why didn't he show the slightest trace of *interest,* let alone jealousy? Was it just emo-tional lethargy? It was possible. It was quite possible . . . Or was his composure based on some sort of *knowledge?* Was it possible, Jasmin asked herself, aghast, that Roland knew things about Lacy which she herself didn't?

I'll go out and fetch your prescription in a minute, he said.

Thanks, Roland. I . . . I'm very grateful for all this, for everything you're doing . . . (Jasmin hesitated before going on.) I think Lacy poisoned me on purpose, you know. He

197

set it up. He took me to a place where he *knew* it would happen . . .

Oh, come on now, said Roland, laughing openly at her.

He made me eat tepid chili, Jasmin said in the same slow voice. He didn't eat any of it himself. Well, hardly any. He *knew*.

Roland looked around the room for an ashtray. When he couldn't find one, he tipped the ash from his cigarette out of the open window. I can't see how he can have *made* you eat anything. He didn't force it down your throat, did he? And anyway, what possible good would it have done him?

Jasmin picked at the duvet. He's not with me at all on this, she thought, He's nowhere near me on this. Why won't he see? And it was making her feel uncomfortable.

Why do you keep giving Lacy the benefit of the doubt? she said. You're sounding like my mother. He can't put a foot wrong for her either. It seems as if it's only me who sees how weird he is. Just listen now, just listen . . .

And breathlessly, sketchily, she told Roland about the trip to Wales, the dreams, the singing, about how Lacy had more or less told her that old Alice was going to die, about his refusal to sleep with her, about the virtual breakup of the Piast family. It came out muddled and inconsequential, but there could be no doubt at all that Jasmin intended it to sound conclusive.

Roland rounded on her when she'd finished. Jasmin, he said, This Lacy is just someone you've got too fond of. Can't you see that? He's a bit out of the ordinary, I'll grant you. And he *looks* . . . I don't know, strange. But as far as I can tell, that's about as far as it goes. And—well, this might sound rude—but I'm getting a bit cheesed off with all this stuff about him singling you out . . . engineering chaos in your life. I mean, why should he bother? What's so special about *you*?

Yes, said Jasmin, smiling hotly. What is so special about me?

She'd wanted Roland to loosen up a little. But now that he had, in his own highly reasonable way, it had unsettled her. He still wasn't getting angry for the right reasons. He wasn't getting angry in the way Jasmin wanted.

Hesitantly she tried a different tack. I don't really understand you, Roland, she said. Those . . . those people who came to dinner at your flat, they told me about your wife . . .

They usually do, he sighed, turning back to the window. They usually do.

I'm terribly sorry, honestly I am. It must have been awful for you. And I hate to bring it up like this. But why didn't you tell me? Why didn't you share it with me? It's as if you just shut things out, things you don't want to face. Like Lacy.

Roland tossed his cigarette out of the window. That's a lot of cock, Jasmin. I don't talk about Sarah because there's nothing to say about all that. Nothing that makes me feel any happier. Not now. Why should I go out of my way to make myself *less* happy? . . . (He paused to collect himself, and went on more quietly.) I suppose I'd have told you eventually. So what? What does it matter? And what do you want me to do about this Lacy? Tear my hair out? Tear *your* hair out?

Jasmin closed her eyes and spoke as if the words were hatching themselves one by one inside her head: You're not seeing the weirdness in Lacy because you don't dare. (She turned her face to the wall.) I'm not saying that that's *bad* in itself. It's probably a very sensible way of dealing with things.

Roland put his hands in his trouser pockets and jangled some loose change. Jasmin snatched a furtive look at him. He seemed somehow *larger* than before, less biddable.

Or is it, Jasmin persisted, or is it that you know something that I don't know, about Lacy? Is that what's making you so . . . so bored, by the whole thing?

Roland walked across to the door. Lacy's a bloke, Jasmin, he said. He's just a bloke. If what you say is true, he tells lies. But so what? We all tell lies. Okay, so I've only talked to him twice, but I didn't see anything *threatening* about him. I'll tell you this straight if you want to know, I felt a bit sorry for him. Look at how *tense* you are all the time. Haven't you considered that you might make *him* nervous?

I had, actually, said Jasmin, staring into Roland's face.

He twisted the door handle back and forth. He seemed to be on the brink of saying something difficult, something that would hurt.

Look, he said, I'm going to the chemist's. But he stayed where he was. I think I could love you, Jasmin, he said to the door. I might even love you already. You can tell me to get lost if you like, you can say it's none of my business, but I think you ask the wrong questions about people. Really. (He threw a glance in her direction and smiled, sadly.) And you take yourself far too bloody seriously. It doesn't do you any good. It doesn't do anyone any good.

Now, thought Jasmin, quaking, when he'd gone, Now where have I heard all *that* before?

And then it came to her, clear and pulsing: Roland is involved in this, too, all of it. Somehow or other, Roland is tied up with Lacy. They're together.

33

JASMIN RECOVERED SLOWLY. IT WAS A COUPLE OF DAYS BEFORE she felt strong enough to get up and stay up. So, as she lay in bed, she had plenty of time to read, and plenty of time to think.

Roland spent several hours a day in the room with her. Usually he sat at her worktop, preparing his lessons for the coming school term. Jasmin had almost forgotten that he was a teacher as well as a writer. She'd never properly digested the fact in the first place. There was so much about Roland that she hadn't inspected too closely, so much.

Roland made her some suitable meals. Soups, toast, nothing too heavy. He took away her sicked-on duvet and washed it in his own machine. They didn't speak again about Lacy.

What *is* so special about me? Jasmin thought on the second evening. Why is Roland doing all this for me? I've been nothing but a burden to him ever since we met.

I don't understand why you take so much trouble with me, she said to him later, when he climbed into bed with her.

He took off his glasses, folded them, and placed them on the occasional table beside the phone. There's never any simple answer to that, is there? he said.

No, thought Jasmin, Perhaps there isn't.

The next day, while Roland was away buying books in the city, Jasmin made a decision and acted on it immediately.

I'm leaving, she told the boys, who were sunning themselves on the lawn.

She hadn't seen any of them since telling Roland to get them out of the bathroom. She could no longer look them in the eye. Not now. Not after that scene with Lacy at the party. Not after they'd seen her stripped and vomiting in another man's arms. She just couldn't live with people who had reason to laugh at her. Good reason.

She went back to her room and sat by the window. She'd acted imprudently, she knew that. Now she had just three weeks to find somewhere new. And she couldn't afford anywhere better than the room she already had. But there hadn't been any real option. She had to make a move. She had to get out.

Circumspectly she picked up the jiffy bag that contained Roland's story. Two nights before she'd asked him to read it to her in bed. He'd refused. Jasmin had found that rather strange. In fact she had always been perplexed by Roland's attitude to his writing. Even at the beginning, when it was all they had in common, he hadn't seemed keen to talk about it. Perhaps it was just his modesty. Perhaps it was natural embarrassment. But Jasmin couldn't help feeling that Roland didn't really want her to read his story.

She tore the jiffy bag open. So this is it, she thought, her eyes on the bulletin board. This is the end of my sabbatical season. If I'd carried on working, none of this might ever have happened.

She flicked through the typescript. The story wasn't very long. Fifty pages, if that, neatly printed out by a word processor. It was called *The Children of Llŷr*. A single typeset page was stapled to the top sheet. In the covering letter Lawrence explained that this was the standard introductory section which led the reader into each story in the series. She cast her eyes over it.

Welcome to the twilight world, it began. *This is the place, where land meets sea, where night meets day . . .*

Jasmin swallowed hard. She tried to read the rest one sentence at a time, but her eyes raced on ahead.

Draw closer to the fire now. This is the place. The place where nothing is quite as it seems. Look. Listen. This is where the powers from the otherworld break through. They come from the world behind our own, bringing what they bring. They take and they give. They come then they go. And where they have passed, nothing remains unchanged.

This is the twilight time. A time of true marvels. The old, old, Britain is fading up into the new. Here are the deities, here are the heroes. Our land becomes their land. It is rare that we see them. But they are with us always. They are watching us always. We cannot live without them. They come to us on the back of the truth.

Come, warm your hands at the red past of this island, open up to the otherworld . . .

203

Jasmin took a deep breath.

Welcome to the twilight world . . . She read it through again, this time much more slowly. *They are watching us always. We cannot live without them. They come to us on the back of the truth* . . .

She looked across at the little clay dragon. All right, she said tremulously, all right . . .

And she read Roland's story straight through to the end.

34

IT WAS, OF COURSE, THE FULL VERSION OF THE STORY THAT
Lacy had told Jasmin in Wales.

Roland's version was a good one. He'd made the characters sharp and believable. His style was simple without
being naive or mannered. And it was a quite gripping tale.
In broad outline, it went like this: Branwen was a beautiful
British princess, the sister of giant king Bran. Bran gave
her in marriage to the king of Ireland. But marital discord
followed, and the discord led to open war between Britain
and Ireland. In the end, the two great armies virtually an-
nihilated each other, and Branwen died of grief, because she
had been at the center of so much turmoil.

The story, however, didn't end there. In fact the most haunting episode was still to come.

A mere seven of King Bran's men survived the war. Bran himself had been mortally wounded. The names of the survivors were listed. Naturally enough one of those names was Taliesin. Jasmin had expected as much. At last she was beginning to understand.

She understood that Taliesin would always survive. She understood that death meant nothing, that death—for Taliesin—was just a means to an end, a prelude to another rebirth. On and on, dying and returning, on to the end of time.

The seven men cut off Bran's head and took it from Wales to be buried inside the White Mount in London. It was while they were journeying to London that they came to the island of Gwales in Penfro, to the palace with the forbidden door.

Eighty years went by. But it seemed like eighty minutes. All their memories of sadness and suffering slipped from their minds. These were the fourscore years of forgetfulness. Often Taliesin and the six others looked at the closed door which faced toward Cornwall, and often they wondered what might lie behind it. But not one of them felt the need to open it.

Then at last, on a sunlit morning, one of the seven became too curious. "Shame on me forever," he said, "if I don't open that door and see what I can see!"

He strode up to the door and pulled it back. There, before him, was the glittering sea. And, beyond that, there lay the land of Cornwall.

The six others gathered behind him and looked out too.

As they looked, memory came crashing back to them like a single overwhelming wave. Every sorrow they had ever suffered, every loss of a friend or relative, every cause for grief—all, all came surging back. And with such force, such power! It was as if, in that one brief moment, they were enduring whole lifetimes of pain and anguish . . .

Jasmin shuffled the pages together and carefully slipped them back inside the jiffy bag.

So . . . she thought, I'm there. Now I'm where I need to be.

What else was there to think? She knew that it couldn't last, but at that particular moment she felt nerveless, almost placid. She smiled to herself, knowingly, as if she were practicing a smile in a mirror, a smile for someone else. Then she picked up the phone.

Lawrence, she said, it's about this story you sent me.

Roland King's story, yes? Have you read it now?

I have . . . said Jasmin, still waiting for the storm to break inside her. I was wondering, Lawrence, why you were all so keen for me to illustrate it. I mean, why me in particular? Was it just because I'm cheap?

Lawrence didn't answer at once. Jasmin, he said patiently, I wish you wouldn't do yourself down so. Cost has nothing to do with it. You're a good artist. A very good one.

Thank you, said Jasmin. But who put me up for this job? You?

Lawrence delayed again before answering. As it happens, it was the author himself. He'd seen and liked some of your previous work—you know, the covers—and he suggested you for his story. That's the long and the short of it. Really. We *all* thought you'd do a good job. We imagined you'd enjoy it, too. Personally I thought it might be just the thing to get you back in harness. This sabbatical business isn't going to do you any good in the long run, you know . . .

Jasmin had stopped listening halfway through. So it was
Roland who got me involved? she said. He was the one who
suggested me to the publishers—because he'd liked my previous work? That's what you're saying, right?

Yes. Why?

I just wanted to know, Lawrence. That's all. I'll be in
touch.

An hour or so later, Roland came back from the city
center with his parcel of books. He also had a plastic bag
filled with food from a delicatessen and a bottle of wine.
We could go to the park, he suggested, and have a picnic.

We could, said Jasmin. She was standing by the window
with the little dragon in her hands. We could . . .

She was finding it difficult to focus her eyes. She felt as
if whole layers of her were beginning to peel themselves
away from her essential core. Once I start on this, she
thought with curious lucidity, once I begin, I'll end up on
my own, completely on my own. And then I'll be even less
than I've made myself so far . . . But, because Jasmin was
the girl that she was, she went ahead regardless.

I understand, she said, That it was you who suggested
that I should do the pictures for your story?

That's right, said Roland, his expression caught between
a frown and a smile. I'd seen some of those covers you did.
I liked your figure work. Yes, I put your name to the editor.
I thought I'd told you that?

Jasmin nodded. As a matter of fact you didn't. Anyway
. . . You'd seen *me* before, too, hadn't you? You told me
you'd seen me before, on that first evening. You said we'd
been introduced. So you knew who I was?

Yes, yes, said Roland, settling the bag of food on the
floor and placing his books on the worktop. He looked at

her in bewilderment. What's this about, Jasmin? What's happened? . . .

What were you after, Roland? Tell me. Was it me as an illustrator? Or just me?

Roland smiled slowly. His face had colored up. Suddenly he looked very young. Very young and very attractive. Oh, God, he said. The questions! The questions!

He scratched his beard, then pulled off his glasses and buffed them. He looked hard at Jasmin, but she spoke back to him with no part of herself. If I'm honest, he said eventually, replacing his glasses, If I'm completely honest, I'm not really sure what the answer is. I mean . . . Either. Both. You. I really don't know. But it's not so terrible, is it? It's not important that I was a bit devious? Not now?

Jasmin's face seemed to have died. She placed the dragon back on her music center, then turned and stared at him. He looked so helpless. Young and so helpless. Somewhere inside her she registered the helplessness of him. But she mistrusted what she was seeing, and she said nothing.

Look, he said, flustered now. What's going on here? You should feel flattered. I admired you as an artist— enough to want you to do my book. And I fancied you as . . . as a woman. Perhaps you think I should have given you some sort of affidavit at the start? Look, if it'll make you feel any better, don't read the story. Just forget about it. We can pretend there never was a story, okay?

She looked straight through him. We can't do that, she said solemnly, Because I've already read it. I read it just now, while you were out.

Oh? said Roland, clearly taken off guard. What did you think then?

Lacy told me exactly the same story, Jasmin said levelly. Lacy told me that story just a couple of days before I got your typescript from Lawrence. He took me to Wales, Roland, he took me to the coast, he showed me that island with the three doors, and he told me your story . . .

Oh, Jesus Christ! said Roland. (He had closed his eyes and seemed, without moving a muscle, to have crumpled where he stood.) Not *bloody* Lacy again! I thought we'd finished with all that, you and me? I thought we'd had all that out . . .

The same story! Jasmin screeched at him, taking one step forward, her face fizzing into life at last. It was the same story! You want to call that a coincidence? How many stories are there in the world? The same story, Roland!

Roland looked at the ceiling, the walls, at Jasmin. Stiffly he held out his arms to her in supplication. But what does it *prove*? Eh? What am I supposed to be thinking now? Tell me.

It's not what *you're* supposed to be thinking, said Jasmin, retreating into herself again. It's me. What am *I* supposed to think? And I'll tell you. I'll tell you what I think. I think you're in this with Lacy. Whether you're aware of it or not, I think you're in it right up to your neck . . .

Jasmin! Roland began to move towards her. His face was a picture of anguish. Jasmin, please . . .

Stay there! Jasmin cried. Don't come near me. Don't! Not now. I know you'll say I've got it wrong. I know what you'll say. But I know what I know, Roland. I know what I *feel*, and I've got to believe in that. If I don't there's nothing left. Nothing.

Roland shook his head ruefully. He turned, picked up a pencil from the worktop, and drew some interlocking circles on Jasmin's pad. I'm worried about you, Jasmin, he said. I think you might be having some sort of a breakdown.

Is that so? said Jasmin with a look of contempt. Well

I'm worried about you, too. I'm worried about me being *fixed up* with you. It's so neat. It ties up the loose ends so neatly. It's just what *everyone* wants. But I'm being *pushed*, Roland, and I don't like being pushed.

Roland put down the pencil. I wish you'd stop, he said quietly.

But Jasmin wouldn't stop. Instead she began to cry. Sudden, apparently independent tears they were, tears which bubbled up out of her and accompanied rather than interrupted her tirade.

I'm way out of my depth, she sobbed. It's all going on so far away from me and I can't begin to understand it. I don't know if it's me who's conjured Lacy up or if it's you. But he's orchestrated everything down to the last detail. Alice, Kate, Eileen, Sidney . . . And now there's me. The last detail. The finishing touch. And I'm being orchestrated into being with *you*. Don't look at me like that, Roland! You know it's true! He's come at me from God knows where, Roland, and wherever he's been, nothing remains unchanged—isn't that the way it goes? *Isn't* it?

Roland picked up his parcel of books. He looked at her curiously. I'm not sure I'm with you, he said. His voice was shaky with frustration. I just can't believe I'm hearing this.

Jasmin folded her arms and turned to the window. One of the boys on the lawn saw her and waved. Lacy won't have me, she said, still crying, Because he's leaving me to you. That's why you've never regarded him as any kind of threat. That's why you've never been jealous of him. I've seen through this thing, Roland. And as long as it's in me to hold out, I want no part of it. I want no part of it.

Jasmin heard Roland opening her door. You're telling me to go? he asked.

211

Jasmin didn't look round. But she said the words and she regretted them even as she spoke: I'm telling you to go.

You can't carry on like this, he said, almost skittishly. You can't keep it up.

Jasmin waited to hear her door closing but the sound didn't come. Roland cleared his throat and spoke again.

In the light of everything else, he said, I don't suppose this is exactly crucial . . . And we may not even be talking about the same island . . . But as I understood it, you can't actually *see* Gwales from the Welsh coast.

And Jasmin, who hadn't been sure whether she had seen an island or not, thought only of Lacy—a man who simply *knew*, a man whose knowing had penetrated her and her entire world and then passed far beyond her.

I should think, she said without turning, That Lacy would know what he was talking about.

And when Roland was out of her house, Jasmin did the next thing.

She phoned Lacy.

35

JASMIN LOST COUNT OF THE NUMBER OF TIMES SHE TRIED TO reach Lacy that day. The oaf answered the phone once. Every other time it was the middle-aged woman. The woman whom Lacy had called Carol. The pregnant landlady. She was unusually patient. Each time, she promised Jasmin that she would ask Lacy to ring back if and when he came in. More than that, she kept reminding Jasmin, she couldn't do.

Eventually, late in the evening, Jasmin fell into conversation with her.

We can't go on meeting like this, said the woman, with

a ripe laugh. I know who *you* are, but why don't I introduce myself? My name's Carol.

You're Lacy's landlady? Jasmin asked dubiously.

I am. Although I don't feel like it nowadays. The man's hardly ever here.

Jasmin said nothing. It had startled her to find that Lacy had been telling the truth about something. And it had undermined her, too.

I hope you won't think I'm interfering, said Carol, But aren't you the girl who had that set-to with Terence at the party?

(Terence? thought Jasmin. *Terence?*)

Yes, she said, I'm very sorry about that . . .

No, no. I didn't mean for you to apologize. It's just that, well, I've been thinking about you. Are you . . . Are you in some kind of trouble?

No, said Jasmin. Well, yes . . .

They both laughed. An awkward silence followed.

In all honesty, said Carol, I can't see Terence coming back here tonight. But tomorrow . . . I think he said he's got someone coming to stay tomorrow. Why don't you pop around at tea time? You can wait for him here. Then if he doesn't show up, well, we could have a chat anyway.

Jasmin frowned at the receiver. Why was this woman playing the Good Samaritan with her? It didn't feel right. It didn't feel right at all. But it *would* take her a step closer to Lacy. That was all that mattered now. Pride, emotional competence, even rational thought—these were just things of the past.

That's very kind of you, she said quickly. Yes, all right. Thank you.

Good, said Carol, But on second thoughts, don't come

out for tea. Wait till I've got the boys out of the way. Come for a drink. Around half seven?

Jasmin had to ask Carol for the address. When she'd jotted it down, she said, without detectable self pity, I've known him for two months and he hasn't even told me where he lives.

Well, did you ever ask him? said Carol. He's not a particularly secretive kind of person, is he?

That night, Jasmin drank gin before going to bed. A lot of gin. She didn't want to lie awake thinking for too long.

Carol had been right to put that last question to her. She *hadn't* ever asked Lacy where he lived. She'd simply presumed that he wouldn't tell her, and she'd wanted to spare herself one more round of humiliation.

Had she been unfair to him? Was he *really* what she thought he was? After all, he'd given her his phone number readily enough . . . It didn't bear thinking about. None of it. Here I am, thought Jasmin, a tense woman alone in a small dark room, and I want him so cruelly badly.

Deeper into the night, she found herself trying to remember a moment, any moment, when she'd felt really happy with Lacy. Frantically she ransacked her recent memory and she came up with nothing. She'd been happy, both actively and passively, with Roland. But with Lacy she had been constantly dogged by doubt, suspicion, trepidation, shame . . . not to mention boredom. Lacy didn't even hold out the *possibility* of happiness. I never saw myself as a woman like this, she thought. I don't understand the nature of the challenge, so how can I be expected to respond to it? How? . . .

Then, mercifully, she slept, and just before waking she dreamed that she was back in the palace. This time the palace was different. It seemed smaller, more like a house. A comfortable house. A family house. And there was no sunlight at the two open doorways. Through the doorway to her right she could see suitcases, a curtainless window, a few sticks of furniture. Through the one to her left she could see Lacy, hunched on the edge of a bed, working at that gargoyle with his knife. He didn't look up. *The wrong door,* Jasmin told herself. *The wrong door . . .* She felt so happy, so light, so relieved.

The singing seemed to be enveloping her, and it was coming from behind the locked door. She reached for the handle of the door, but this time she didn't touch it. She didn't know what was behind the door and she didn't care. Not now. She dropped her hand to her side.

The singing was taking hold of her. It's happening, she thought, It's going to be all right. I believe it. I'm going to be all right.

She was being lifted. She was floating slowly upwards. The singing was bearing her up and out of the darkness. Sunlight now, above and around her. She looked down and there was no palace. Only sea, and land—an island and, beyond that, the shores of an infinite land mass. This is the place, said a voice, where the land meets the sea . . . And he was beside her. His hand was cool against her temple. Roland. Roland . . .

When she opened her eyes, the first thing she saw was the dragon. It was some distance away, up there on the music center, but it seemed to be dominating the entire room. A sunlit little room, still ringing with voices, jubilant voices.

Stop it! Jasmin shouted aloud, throwing her hands over her ears. Stop it! Stop it! Stop it!

Then she heard the little girl outside, squealing, giggling.

Jasmin sprang from the bed. She pulled on her dressing gown and she snatched up the dragon. Now, she said to its face. Now . . .

She skipped down the stairs. One of the boys was cleaning a pair of cricket boots in the kitchen. He watched Jasmin walk straight through to the garden in her bare feet. There was still a sheet of dew on the grass. Through the beech hedge she could see the girl and, further back, her mother. The girl was wearing a red one-piece swimsuit.

Hey, said Jasmin, rustling the leaves to attract her attention. Hello! Look, I've got something for you. Do you like dragons?

She could see only the girl's face now, her face and the top of her chest. She looked doubtfully at Jasmin, too shy to move, either forward or backward.

Here, Jasmin said breathlessly, I want you to have this. She pushed the little dragon through the hedge. He's a lucky dragon. I don't need him any more. I'd like you to have him—if you want him.

The girl wrinkled her face. Then she came forward, and took the dragon in both hands. She looked at it, disappointed, as though she'd been expecting it to perform in some way.

He's just a dragon, said Jasmin, trying to keep smiling. She couldn't think of anything else to tell her.

What do you say? said a voice close by, the voice of the girl's mother. Say thank you to the lady.

Thank. You, the girl duly repeated, before dashing out of sight with her new toy.

Jasmin went back indoors, back up the stairs on her wet feet.

Her room seemed airier when she got back. Emptier,

but indisputably easier to breathe in, to *be* in. Jasmin looked out of the window.

The girl was lying on her stomach now, propped up on her elbows. She'd placed the indestructible dragon right in front of her nose, and was happily whispering her own sort of gibberish to it.

What have I done? thought Jasmin. Oh, what have I done?

But she knew. She understood. She knew that she had given away so much more than a little dragon.

She had parted with what Lacy had told her to keep. She had, she knew, surrendered any hold that she still had on Lacy himself. She had freed him, effectively, to continue along his endless path of death and birth.

But even if he's got to move on, Jasmin told herself, there's no reason why he shouldn't take me with him. There's nothing, no one, not even Roland, for me to stay for. Not now. Not here. And I just can't take any more.

36

Jasmin found the street well before half-past seven. It was twenty minutes walk away from where she lived herself. She strolled past the house several times, looking it up and down from the opposite pavement.

It was a three-storied house with a basement. Several bicycles were leaning against the garden wall. It looked like a student house, comfortably dilapidated. It didn't seem like a family house at all. It wasn't what Jasmin had been expecting.

He might be in there now, she thought, Inside a room, behind a door, sitting in a chair, eating a plate of food, surrounded by walls, *his* walls. *Him.*

She knew that he wanted her to be there that evening. She knew there was nothing impromptu about this. Lacy had guided her to his digs as surely as he'd guided the rest of her family into the wilderness and then back out of it. And the woman Carol was immaterial. Jasmin hadn't come to talk, she hadn't come to listen. Something beyond words was waiting for her inside that welcoming house. Something conclusive. A means to an end.

In the day of trouble, I shall be of more use to you than three hundred salmon. Jasmin's day of trouble had been lasting for the whole of her sabbatical season. This had to be where it ended. And Jasmin was ready. She was more than ready. She was just longing for it to be over.

It was still only seven-fifteen. Jasmin walked into the adjoining road and stared at the shop windows. She was wearing a blue pinafore dress and espadrilles. She'd taken some time over her hair and makeup, and she was pleased with her reflection. In the dark glass she couldn't see anything wrong with her at all. *There's nothing wrong with the way you look,* he'd said. He'd been right about so much else. Why not that, too? Why not that?

When she returned to Carol's street, four smart cars were moving to a halt. They were moving very slowly, the way cars move when only the one in front knows where it's going. They all drew up close to Carol's house. Jasmin stood and watched.

Eight, nine, ten people clambered out on to the pavement. Men and women in their forties, laughing confidently, the men in dinner jackets, the women in beautiful expensive gowns. They were calling out to one another like drunken teenagers, people who'd given themselves something to celebrate. One by one they trooped into a house several doors up from Carol's.

220

When they'd gone, Jasmin tried to think of a time when she herself had been that happy. But, to her annoyance, all she could remember was the swimming pool, jumping off the high springboard at the swimming pool. Only that. A solitary, easy to miss moment of bliss. A happiness that had excluded everyone but herself.

And she knew then that she had never been happy with anyone else. Not happy in the way that people like, say, Kate or the boys or even Eileen were occasionally happy. Why? she thought, with more interest than resentment. Why?

She knocked on Carol's door and the oaf answered.

Jasmin smiled as he ushered her in. That's right, he said, with the voice which she had refused to believe in, The old girl said she was expecting someone. She's in the kitchen, mate, up the stairs there. He was wearing a Sony Walkman, and he spoke rather more loudly than he needed to.

He was young, less than twenty, and his features were impossibly sharp, as if someone with a set of tools was still working on them. He could well have been one of Lacy's friends from the pub on that first Sunday. By the time Jasmin had climbed the stairs to the first-floor kitchen, he had disappeared.

Will gin do you? Carol asked over her shoulder.

She was standing at a work surface, chopping cabbage. She continued to prepare various vegetables throughout the entire conversation, looking up once or twice, tilting her head to smile. Jasmin guessed that she was the kind of woman who never stopped, the kind of woman who was only too glad to dispense no-nonsense advice to the less busy, the less committed.

He . . . He's not here, I suppose? asked Jasmin.

221

No, that's right. He's gone to the station. To collect someone.

A girlfriend?

Ah, now that's a moot point with our Terence. We've never actually seen him with one of those! (She poured Jasmin some gin, added a splash of tonic and handed her the glass.) He seems to spend most of his time with the boys.

Your sons, you mean?

Oh, no, she laughed. Young men, you know? Good-looking lads in the main.

Jasmin felt as if she'd been filleted. What are you saying? she heard herself asking.

I'm not saying anything, Carol told her, looking up and smiling pointedly. I'm not saying anything at all.

Oh, God, help me, thought Jasmin, Oh, God, God help me . . .

The kitchen was huge and it looked filthy. Carol herself was none too tidy. She was a big woman, handsome in a square-jawed, Slavic kind of way, and the look of pregnancy seemed to suit her. But the smock she was wearing was streaked with grease, and her dark hair, which had been knotted back prettily at the party, now hung all over her face. She could have been no more than a year or two older than Jasmin. But beside her Jasmin felt sketchy, unfocussed, adolescent.

What else do you know about Lacy? Jasmin said, knowing that it was unnecessary to ask, pointless to ask.

Well, he's leaving us. He's going somewhere up north. You knew that, did you?

Jasmin blinked. He . . . He did say something, yes. (I could go, too, she thought immediately. Not up north though. I could go where he's *really* going. I'm ready. He doesn't have to go without me. *He's got to take me with him.*)

He's off at the weekend. We'll be sorry to lose him, but as I say, we've hardly seen him recently . . . You don't know anyone who wants a room, do you?

No, said Jasmin firmly, No I don't. (I shouldn't be humoring her, she thought. I shouldn't be doing this. She's a part of it. Her and her baby. He's using her just like he's been using all the others.)

Did you tell Lacy I was coming? Jasmin said.

I did mention it, yes. That was all right, wasn't it?

Oh, I don't mind. Did he . . . say anything?

About you, you mean? Carol heaved a pile of chopped cabbage to one side, pulled across a colander full of peas and began to shell them. Well, obviously, I asked him about you after that party . . .

And?

Carol breathed out heavily. He said you weren't very happy. And he said you kept on trying to make yourself unhappier.

You all speak the same way, thought Jasmin. He's made you all speak the same way. She stared hard at a torn poster, of Venice, just above the kitchen sink. I won't cry here, she told herself, I *won't* . . .

He likes you very much, Carol went on. He told me so. After the party, and again this afternoon . . . He'd like you to be happier, really. I don't know what it is with him exactly: he seems to feel this sort of responsibility for people, sometimes people he doesn't even know . . . He's awfully sweet.

Sweet, Jasmin repeated, nodding her head. (She'd put down her gin and tonic, and was walking, slowly, around the great pine table, pointing her toes in front of her as she went. She was imagining Lacy, clean in this dirty place,

223

talking, laughing, helping . . . organizing.) Why did you invite me here? she said. Did he tell you to invite me?

Carol looked at the wall for a moment. Not in so many words, she said. I don't think he minds me talking to you, though. I'm sure he'd have said if he did. Personally, I've always found him to be a very straightforward kind of boy.

Jasmin nodded, amused. And did he tell you to suggest to me that he was a queer?

I didn't suggest anything of the sort, Carol said mildly. She went back to her peas. The kitchen clock chimed eight.

No, said Jasmin quietly. Of course you didn't.

There was nothing to be gained from talking to Carol. It wasn't even worth offending her. Jasmin could trust no one but herself. She alone seemed able to sense who Lacy was, *what* Lacy was. And how, in all honesty, could she expect a woman like Carol to see his *otherness*? But she had to take the initiative, once again, just to make sure for herself.

Can I see his room? she said.

Carol at last turned away from the work surface. She rubbed her hands on her smock and grinned. *What?*

Can I have a look inside his room? Please. You can come with me. I won't touch anything. I just want to see. I just want . . . to see.

Carol laughed. She pushed the hair back out of her face. From the front she didn't look pregnant at all. Well, I don't think there *is* anything to see actually, she said. I heard him packing this afternoon. And he really didn't have much stuff in there in the first place . . .

Please, said Jasmin. Just two minutes. Just . . . just so that I can know.

Carol laughed again and swayed across to the door. Come on then, she said as if to a child. It'll have to be quick, though. I don't want him finding us in his room when he gets back from the station.

Jasmin followed her down one flight of stairs, then another. Both our lodgers live in the basement, Carol explained. They don't get bothered by the kids' noise down here, you see. (She pointed to one of two doors. It was closed.) That's George's room, the young man who let you in. And this is where Terence occasionally deigns to spend a night . . .

Lacy's door was ajar. Jasmin had known that it would be. Slightly ajar, just like the door to Kate's room at her parents' house. Another wrong door to go through. But she had to do it. He wanted her to go through this one. He *wanted* her to.

And so she did.

37

No one could have called it a cosy room.

Even if Lacy hadn't packed his personal belongings into the two suitcases under the window, no one could have called it cosy in there. It was small, smaller than Jasmin's own room. There were no curtains, no carpets, the walls were nothing but off-white plaster.

Jasmin took two steps forward. On the other side of the bed, a small portable cassette player was standing on the floorboards, along with a stack of tapes. There was a rancid smell in that room, a body smell that she hadn't come across before. And it was shot through with the stink of turpentine or linseed oil, and rotting fruit, and fish.

There was just the minimum of furniture. A single bed, a chest of drawers, a bare rail full of coat hangers, a waste bin. It was more of a large cupboard than a room. Yet a man paid money to be here. The most important man in Jasmin's life. It was from here that Terence Lacy had honed in on her and taken her family to pieces.

Carol hadn't followed Jasmin into the room. She stood in the doorway, keeping an ear open for the sound of Lacy's key unlocking the front door. (You needn't worry, Jasmin wanted to tell her. You needn't pretend to be worried. He won't come back until it's time. He won't come back until I've done whatever it is that he wants me to do.)

It doesn't smell too good, does it? Carol laughed.

Jasmin shook her head. It's awful, she said. What is it?

I think it's mainly the solutions he puts on those little wooden models of his.

Little models?

You know, figurines. Little figures. He's awfully good. Miniatures they are really. He does people from history— Charles I, Alexander the Great, Boadicea, that kind of thing. He's done people from the Bible as well, and characters from old myths and legends. He does them in lots of different woods . . . So he didn't tell you about that, then?

Jasmin just smiled, thinly.

Ah. Well all sorts of people commission him. Apparently he can ask up to a hundred quid a time for a model, a hundred and twenty-five even. It's a lucrative business. I've known him to make two in an evening!

So . . . So that's his work then? That's what he does for a living?

Well he sometimes helps out this friend of his who runs a scaffolding firm. Oh, and he does up second-hand cars occasionally, with another friend. But yes, the models are his main line of work. There, she said pointing, Over there in the bin. It looks as if he's thrown a few of them away . . .

Thus it was Carol who directed Jasmin to the carvings. If Jasmin hadn't been prompted, she would probably have withdrawn from that foul-smelling room as quickly as possible. It was Carol who sent her to forage in Lacy's wastebin. Carol. Lacy's pregnant landlady.

And it was all there on the top. Lying amid a squalid mess of pear cores, congealed rice and lumps of meat, beer bottles, rags, ashes, and coils of mouldering vegetable peel. It was all there. What Jasmin had been meant to find.

She squatted down, averting her head from the stench, and reached out with stiff arms to pick off first the carvings, then the torn fragments of the photographs.

Oh, I say, cried Carol, coming into the room now, I wouldn't touch anything in there if I were you. It looks absolutely disgusting . . . Oh, my *God*!

She put her hand to her mouth when she saw what Jasmin was turning in her hands. A carving, a hideous leering female figure, its face almost as big as the rest of its body, its hands reaching down behind either knee, and pulling open a vast vagina.

My God, said Carol, I didn't know he went in for that sort of thing, too. (Jasmin glanced up at her. Carol was narrowing her eyes to stop herself from smiling.) But I've seen photos of something quite similar, she went on. A kind of fertility thing it was. In a church somewhere. Dear me though, that really is *vile*.

I think I saw him making it, said Jasmin, softly, calmly. It's my sister. (To Jasmin, Kate's features were unmistakable in the caricatured face. The high forehead, the wide eyes, the hollowed-out cheeks, even the hair—wet hair, hair wet from the bath, hair which Kate had just run her fingers through, slowly.) And this, Jasmin continued, dropping the carving of Kate and picking up one of the others. This is me.

Carol took it from her. So it is, she said admiringly. So it is.

And it was Jasmin in a swimsuit, her legs together and slightly bent, her arms raised like wings. And she was smiling, eyes closed, beatific. Her smile seemed to be saying: Let this go on.

It's *very* good, said Carol, isn't it? A really good likeness. I wonder why he didn't just give it to you, though? Instead of throwing it out?

Jasmin wasn't listening. She was methodically piecing together the soiled pieces of a Polaroid snap on the floorboards. It was her. Her at the swimming pool, pictured in mid air as she leapt from the high springboard.

Aha, said Carol, I see. So he based the model on that picture. You posed for him then?

Jasmin shook her head. She shuffled the other fragments of photo. It was easy enough to imagine the larger wholes. Her, walking at night by the canal. Her, sitting at the window of her room—a shot which seemed to have been taken from a position in the garden next door. Her, walking out of the maternity hospital. Her, her, her . . .

You posed for these, though? said Carol, bending down awkwardly to look closer.

What do you think? Jasmin replied. She knew now, for sure, that she had been posing for Lacy ever since they'd met. I wasn't wrong, she thought. I was right to trust myself. She peered into the waste bin again.

A screwed up sheet of paper had stuck itself to the neck of a beer bottle. There was writing on it. Jasmin plucked it out with thumb and forefinger and began to uncrumple it. This, she knew, is going to be what he wants me to know. And there was just one line.

There is nothing, he had written, *In which I have not been.*

Jasmin read his message twice, then placed the sheet back in the bin.

In front of her on the floor were Lacy's other discarded figures and models: the one of her house—a perfect miniature replica, the one of old Alice in her deck chair, the one of Sidney, dressed as he'd been dressed in old Frank's photo, but with his arm raised, waving. The one of a Cavalier, hairless, quite faceless . . .

Jasmin knelt forward. With inordinate care she loaded everything back into the waste bin. Just as she'd found it. Everything—even the superb little carving of herself. And when she'd finished, she rose unsteadily to her feet. Moments later, she fainted.

38

WHEN JASMIN CAME TO, SHE ACCEPTED AT ONCE THAT SHE WAS dead.

And death is a means to an end! she thought stupidly. *Death is just a means to an end.*

But for almost a minute she didn't dare to open her eyes. The singing seemed to be buoying her up. Loud, relentless, sweet and sad, swarming up at her from another place, draining all the substance and age from her body.

She assumed that she must be floating. But her cheek was resting on a coarse, firm surface, while her feet were pressing against something smoother, harder. She allowed her eyelids to flicker.

It's all right, a voice whispered. A woman's voice, and someone touching her hair, her shoulder. She smelled sweat.

Jasmin opened her eyes. She was curled up on a small, greasy sofa. There was a patch of damp on the worn fabric where she'd been dribbling, open mouthed. Her feet were jammed against the sofa's wooden arm.

The hand was still smoothing her hair. A cool hand, a gentle hand.

Roland? . . . whispered Jasmin.

No, my love, it's Carol. You've been out for several minutes. I got my husband to bring you up here.

Jasmin twisted her head, looked up, and again she knew everything that had happened since she'd arrived in that house. She was back in the vast kitchen, the vast filthy kitchen, back in with all the vegetables, the pine table and the torn poster of Venice.

Carol . . . Carol . . . she said to the sweaty woman, who smiled back.

If you hadn't come round soon we were going to fetch a doctor, said a man wearing a jacket and tie. He was kneeling beside the sofa. Carol introduced him as her husband but Jasmin didn't catch his name.

And then Jasmin realized that the singing hadn't stopped. That Carol was actually raising her voice a little to compete with it.

That sound? . . . said Jasmin. What? . . .

It's our Terence, she said, raising her eyebrows at her husband. He does like a bit of volume to his music.

Jasmin sat up, swinging her feet to the floor. She felt vaguely sick, but as far as she could tell she was otherwise none the worse for wear.

He's back? she said.

That's right, said Carol, He came in almost as soon as we got you up here.

Of course he did, thought Jasmin. Of course he did.

And then she saw the look of pity in Carol's eyes. And from that look, she read everything that she needed to know.

This, at long last, was the vindication. Ever since she'd known Lacy she'd been afraid that this was going to happen. No, no that wasn't right. She'd been afraid for *much* longer than that. This was what she'd been anticipating from the moment she'd started going with men. Anticipating, ever since she'd complied with the first safe boy, anticipating. Then through each of those safe and silly men, anticipating, letting every single one of them do to her what she'd felt it was essential to let them do.

Carol's husband stood and said that he had to get back to his work. He left the kitchen.

Jasmin kept gazing up into Carol's eyes, kept seeing the pity. She knew that Lacy was with Kate. She knew that Lacy was down there in his appalling little room with her sister. Lacy had come back from the station and now he was down there, with Kate.

My sister, she thought. Pregnant. Married. My beautiful rival.

And Jasmin's sister was going to have Lacy. Or perhaps, Kate being Kate, she was having him already. On him. Around him. Reaching for him. In that room. Within those four walls. Doing what she knew so much better than Jasmin how to do. Doing it so well because she really *wanted to do it*. Good old Kate. Filling in a couple of idle days before her husband came to fetch her.

Of course she was down there. She couldn't really have been anywhere else.

I'm sorry . . . said Jasmin. She eased herself up onto her feet. She felt quite steady. Weak, but quite steady. Her eyes were now on a level with Carol's. She was smelling that atrocious smell again, thinking of the waste bin.

You saw it, she said to Carol, because despite it all she wanted Carol to be with her. You saw what he'd done . . .

I saw the pictures and the models, said Carol through half-pursed lips. But I didn't actually see what he'd *done*, no.

Jasmin smiled at her. The singing seemed to be getting louder. She felt nothing for Carol but envy. Envy and a certain amount of awe. There she was, heavy with her baby. One more mother. One more unmitigated woman.

He's been orchestrating my life, Jasmin said, her voice sullen, businesslike. He's been watching me, taking pictures of me, making those, those . . . things, and he's been using them to make my life fall to pieces.

Carol narrowed her eyes. I don't . . . quite get you, she said, beginning to smile.

You don't know who he is, do you? said Jasmin. You can't see, because you don't need to see. You don't understand where he's come from or where he's heading. But I do. I do.

But he's just a bald-headed boy! said Carol. Hey, where are you going now?

Where do you imagine?

Carol took just one step towards her. I wouldn't, you know, she said.

Is that a threat?

Of course it's not a threat. I'm just saying be careful.

Jasmin turned to face her. Careful of what?

Of hurting yourself. Making yourself more unhappy than you already are. (Carol smiled, a broken sort of smile.

Jasmin had seen that expression so often on Eileen.) He's going, he's leaving. He's not for you, my love. What *good* can you do by going back down there now?

But the singing was too strong for Jasmin. The singing, and the fact that she was ready, and her need for more of Lacy. Even like this. *Especially* like this.

She began to descend the first flight of stairs. Carol followed her out on to the landing and watched. It was dark further down in the basement. Jasmin stepped into the shadows. I'm a grown-up girl, she was thinking, And I can't look after myself. I'm a grown-up girl, but now I'm ready . . .

The sound of the singing was almost deafening. She wouldn't have believed that the cassette player could be giving out so much noise. This was the singing. She knew it from St. David's, she knew it from her dreams. A song from the depths. The endless music of an old land rich in knowing. Stay away, it was saying. Don't come near.

Two wrong doors, she murmured, And now this one. Now this one.

And this door was closed. Not like Kate's door at home. Not like this same door just minutes before. This was no invitation to make a mistake. Lacy didn't want her inside. Lacy thought it would be better if she stayed in the dark. Lacy. And what *he* wanted.

And then there's me, Jasmin told herself. Then there's me and what *I* want.

She put her ear to the door. Nothing but the singing. Nothing else in there. But she knew, she knew. She put out her hand and gripped the handle. She turned it slowly. It moved a small way and then it stopped. She tried again. It moved and then it stopped.

In the day of trouble, I shall be of more use to you than three hundred salmon. For a moment, Jasmin believed that Lacy had locked the door. It was only for a moment, but she believed it. And that was long enough to start making the difference.

The singing was getting louder. So loud now that Jasmin stopped thinking coherently. So very loud that she was finding it impossible to remember.

She let her fingers slip from the handle. The singing, sweet and sad and *true,* was cocooning her. She shook her head, she clawed at her memory, but her sadnesses were no longer her own. The song had broken them up, made them small, scoured her clean and distributed them all in places where they couldn't reach her.

All Jasmin could see were seven men huddled in a palace doorway. Seven slow men looking out at what they'd been forbidden to see. Seven men, and among them was Taliesin.

And as they looked, memory came crashing back to them like a single overwhelming wave . . . It was as if, in that one brief moment, they were enduring whole lifetimes of pain and anguish . . .

Jasmin stared at the door handle. She was a vessel brimming with the song. It coursed through her and shone out of her. And there was nothing else inside. Nothing that she recognized.

She smiled at the door handle. Let this go on, she thought. I don't need it to be significantly different from this. This is my side. *I'm* on this side, me. *Roland* and me. I don't have to go with Lacy . . .

And she was back on the bottom stair. She was feeling giddy. The gorgeous music was sweeping her up now, up to the ground floor where Carol was waiting in the light, watching, guessing.

You didn't go in? she said.

236

No, Jasmin replied in airy-headed confusion. He . . .
The door was locked.

The pregnant woman pressed her lips together in a
smile. There isn't a lock on his door, she said with almost
sensual delight. I'm pleased. I'm so pleased for you.

Jasmin walked to the front door.

I can run you back home if you like, Carol called after
her.

No thanks, said Jasmin, pulling the door open and staring at the streetlamp opposite, I'm fine. Really I am.

And she knew that Lacy, having led her so far, was
letting her go. And she knew that he was right. He had to
be right. He had so much on his side.

At last, at long last, there was no difference between
what the two of them wanted.

39

IT WAS JASMIN WHO HAD MADE THE FIRST MOVE, NOT LACY. That was the undeniable truth.

Regardless of everything that had happened afterward, it was Jasmin who'd made the first move. If she hadn't called out to him on that summer afternoon, he would probably have walked straight past. He hadn't given her any kind of encouragement. He hadn't even been looking in her direction.

There was no escaping the fact that Jasmin was the one who'd started it. Sitting up there on her knoll in the park, she'd quite simply summoned Lacy into her life.

And Lacy, for his part, hadn't needed to be asked twice.

He had accompanied her through her sabbatical season, gladly, because that was the kind of man that he was. Just the kind of man that Jasmin had needed, then, in her day of trouble.

But of course it couldn't end there. It wasn't meant to end there.

40

JASMIN WAS IN THE BATHROOM WHEN HER MOTHER RANG, early on Sunday morning. She'd been in there for some time. Her period was late. It had been due on Friday and it was late. This was something that had never happened to Jasmin before. Not once in all her womanhood.

Eileen wanted to know whether Jasmin intended to come to the party with Roland or with Lacy. She had, after all, invited them both.

Neither, Jasmin told her. I'll be on my own.

Ah well, said Eileen. They'll both be welcome anyway.

(Not *they would*, Jasmin noticed, but *they will*. She attached little importance to it. Eileen could say what she liked, now. It didn't matter in the slightest.)

Oh, and I had a letter from Terence, Eileen said. It came yesterday . . .

Terence, thought Jasmin, *Terence* . . .

Well it wasn't what you could call a letter, Eileen went on. Just a note really, to thank me for writing to him. I don't know, he needn't have put himself to the trouble. I wasn't expecting any reply. He's awfully sweet, isn't he?

He is, said Jasmin. What did he say?

Oh, you know, just thank you . . . And then he wrote this little bit of a poem, or a hymn or something. Nice, it was. I'll show it to you when you come.

I'd like to hear it now, said Jasmin. If it's not too much bother? Do you think you could read it out to me, the poem?

Hold on, Eileen told her, I'll fetch it . . . She wasn't gone long. Here, she said, *Be not displeased at thy misfortune . . . While I continue thy protector/Thou hast not much to fear.* Lovely, isn't it?

Umm . . . said Jasmin. Umm . . . I'll see you later.

The party was due to start at one. That was when Michael and the Germans were arriving. Jasmin drove out of the city soon after nine. She was going to be early but that was deliberate. The boys were interviewing for a new tenant again that morning, and she preferred not to be there while the candidates mooched around her room. (Over the past few days she'd grown tired of looking up from her sketches of King Bran and the palace by the sea, smiling at them all, answering their polite questions about why she was moving out. So many people competing for such a paltry little room. So many young people, starting out, in sober clothing.)

She herself had struck lucky at once. An agency had found her a "studio flat," closer in to the city center. It was only a six-month let, but the room was cheap, large and airy. The owner, a widow in her fifties who lived on the premises, was currently taking up Jasmin's references. She'd been delighted to learn that Jasmin illustrated books for a living. So delighted that she'd written off the other prospective tenants on her list without even seeing them. Ah well, Jasmin had thought. Ah well.

She concentrated hard on the road. It was a brisk bright day. A good day for driving. She hadn't brought old Frank's photo this time. But in her bag she had a camera. She wanted someone, preferably not old Frank, to take another family group for her. Sidney wouldn't be in it, of course. Just Eileen and Jasmin and Kate. But it would be something. A record of sorts.

Also in her bag was a copy of Roland's little book, *Radiant Brow*, his story of Taliesin.

It hadn't been easy to get hold of. The main booksellers had sold out of it and were awaiting a reprint. But eventually she'd come across a solitary copy at an esoteric bookstand in the market.

She had read it perhaps six times.

She'd found the text just as enjoyable, just as subtle, as that of Roland's later work—the one that she'd read in typescript. He'd taken it far beyond a simple story of shapeshifting and divine intervention. He had somehow touched on the *transcendence* of Taliesin, his indisputable presence, the *need* for his presence. That editor in the wine bar had been right: These were matters of belief, of unchanging truth.

But Roland had rendered a proportion of his text in the form of Taliesin's poems. And these were the parts that spoke most directly to Jasmin. She could hear Roland's voice in them to be sure, but behind his voice she could hear Lacy declaiming. She really could hear Lacy.

Naturally, one of the poems included a version of the words which Lacy had written to Eileen. A less resonant version, to be sure, but the message was exactly the same.

As long as I am your protector
There is nothing you have to fear . . .

Jasmin believed it. She knew that it was true.

She put her foot down as she drew closer to home. She wished that Sidney was going to be there. But he'd held out, withstanding Eileen's petitions and appeals. He was a proud man, and Jasmin could sympathize with him up to a point. According to Eileen, he'd got most of his travel arrangements sorted out already. He was due to fly home some time in the early autumn. Jasmin wondered how he might look back, then, at the last thirty-odd years of his life. How would he present those years to his older self? How would he come to define them? It was so important, she knew, to have a perspective.

When she reached the house, she said hello to Eileen, Kate, and old Frank, then went straight to the bathroom. It was still no good. She was late and she was staying late.

She came back down and complimented her mother and sister on the way they were looking. She wasn't just being polite either. They looked strikingly similar: two married women, two women who, in their very different ways, would always belong in the world of men.

And several times during the next half hour Jasmin met Kate's eye. Kate looked straight back, giving the impression that there was no reason in the world why she shouldn't.

Jasmin found that strangely reassuring. It was, after all, Jasmin who had chosen not to open Lacy's door. She hadn't actually *seen* Kate. Kate therefore bore no obligation to look penitent. Good luck to you, Jasmin thought. It's better like this. Better for everyone.

And Jasmin was back in the bathroom, wondering, when she heard Lacy's voice.

Then she heard Sidney—and Eileen screaming up the stairs to her, Jas! Jas! Come down, it's Terence! And he's brought your father!

Jasmin began to move very slowly. She presumed that Lacy had come for Kate. It took her almost five minutes to gather herself sufficiently to leave the bathroom. Even then, she could do no more than stand on the landing, and listen to the criss-cross conversations down below.

Sidney's voice was the most prominent. I've come only to see Kate, he was saying repeatedly, as if the words themselves had the power to hold back the avalanche of his history. Only to see Kate. To make up with Kate. Then I will go back to Frank's . . .

And there was Lacy. Lacy was explaining, genially enough, that he really couldn't stay, that he was breaking a journey, that, honestly and truly, he had to be going . . .

Jasmin listened, pressing her hands together, waiting, waiting. Lacy was still talking but she could no longer follow what he was saying. It's not in me to go down there, she thought. Kate was weeping. Tears of relief. She was thanking her father, telling him she loved him. I don't belong among any of that, thought Jasmin, less convinced now. It doesn't concern me any more. I'm on my own.

Jasmin! Eileen yelled again. Quickly, quickly. Terence is taking a photo!

Jasmin's hands moved to her stomach. Perhaps he hasn't

come for Kate, she thought. Perhaps there's something else
. . . She straightened her jacket, swore at herself, and, on
tingling legs, descended the stairs.

From the foot of the staircase she looked through the
open front doorway. Kate, Eileen, Sidney, and old Frank
were standing, with their backs to her, on the doorstep. For
reasons that Jasmin could well imagine, they were all
bunched up together in a space no more than a couple of
feet wide.

Eileen twisted around and beckoned to her. She was
holding up a bouquet of white roses. Look what Terence
brought me! she said, her face popping with excitement.
Come on, hurry up, Jas! You've got to be in the picture
too!

Jasmin prepared her expression and stepped out of the
house. It was still sunny, but a blustery wind was getting
up. When she emerged from behind the close-packed group,
she came face to face with Lacy.

At once he stopped fiddling with his camera, stood to
attention and gave her a salute. There were about ten or
twelve feet between them.

Something out of the ordinary, thought Jasmin. He's here.

He was wearing the jacket and trousers of a generously
cut grey suit, a white T-shirt, and tennis shoes. Jasmin
looked him up and down, smiling. It was like seeing him
for the first time but she didn't have to try very hard to
remember. He's here for me, she told herself. He's not here
for Kate. He's here for me.

She looked into his eyes. There were no shadows. *Something quite out of the ordinary.* There was nothing, she remembered, in which he had not been.

My princess, he called out, bowing to her extravagantly.
Now squeeze in with the rest of them, will you, love? And

we'll get you an even more ridiculous picture than you had the last time round.

Jasmin dutifully put one arm around her mother and another around her father. (How in God's name, she wondered, had Lacy managed to persuade Sidney to come? What could he possibly have *said*?) Kate squatted down in front of them, old Frank peered in from the side.

Jasmin's lips had become very dry. She noticed a rundown Cortina parked on the grass further up the road.

Let's see you smiling then, said Lacy. And the picture was taken.

There we are! he said, stepping up and holding out a Polaroid snap. That's the end of it. (He handed the photo to Eileen.) I hope your party is the most tremendous success. Cheers now then. I really must get moving. All the best, all the very best to you . . .

He's going, Jasmin thought. This *is* going to be the end.

And she watched him clear the low garden wall and walk quickly towards the Cortina. She knew that if she didn't call out to him, on that late summer morning, he would march right out of her life.

Stop! she cried. Lacy! Wait!

She broke away from her family. Wait! she shouted again as she opened the gate on to the road. I know, she called out to him as he turned, I know who you are.

And then she gasped.

41

LACY HAD BEEN TRANSFORMED.

This was no longer the man who had been taking the photo just moments before. This—oh, God!—this was the Lacy that Jasmin had last seen on the canal towpath. His shoulders had dropped, his entire face had tightened. He was looking at her as if she were an accusation made flesh. Jasmin gripped the gatepost, then slowly she moved closer.

And as she approached he changed again. This, now, was the way he had looked in that hotel bar at St. David's— solemn, noble, scoured by the shadows and the sadness of the song.

Behind her Jasmin could hear her family talking excitedly about the photo. They couldn't see what she was seeing. She understood. She knew that they weren't meant to see. And in front of her stood yet another Lacy, the way Jasmin had conjured him twice before, the way he had looked at her in his nakedness, with his penis pointed like a gun, black wells of nothing where his eyes should have been.

Jasmin stood before him and she looked deep into the darkness.

She could feel Lacy's hands beneath her elbows. He was holding her up, stopping her from slumping. The wind blew colder. She smelled the plaster, she felt the brush of his lapel and his cotton T-shirt. Then she steadied herself and embraced him.

Taliesin, she whispered against him. It sounded perfect. It guided her deeper into his arms. He embraced her in return and there was warmth in his caress. This was the body she had craved. This was the flesh.

And she knew this body for what it was: a means to an end, never to be possessed. A means to an end, a medium, enabling him to rise once more from oblivion, freshly defined, like that searing song of the ancients.

Taliesin, she whispered again. It made her feel so calm. She was luxuriating in the calmness he had brought her. The calmness and the strength.

I didn't open your door, she told him softly. I thought I wanted to. I thought I wanted to die with you. But I left the door closed. I want to be happy. I think I can be happy, through you . . .

She felt the pressure of his hands on her back. Those big soft hands. She closed her eyes and nestled her head against his shoulder. There was nothing, nothing, in which he had not been.

I might be pregnant, she said.

Gently he took her shoulders and held her away from him. He was smiling at her. There was a blessing in that smile. But there was more, too—pleasure, tenderness, shrewd amusement—and no surprise. Of course there was no surprise.

Jasmin smiled back at him. She wanted to ask: Why me? Why did you choose me, me and my family? But already she knew why: because she had asked him. There, in the park, when she had needed him, when they had all needed him.

She had asked and he had answered.

They kissed. They drew apart.

Then he simply raised his right hand, saluted, and made for his car. He revved up the engine at once and swerved out recklessly onto the road.

The driver of a truck coming up fast behind sounded his horn but Jasmin scarcely heard it. And then he was gone.

Jasmin felt a hand on her arm. She turned. It was Sidney. Look, he said. Look at this. He handed her the new photo.

It was a good picture, as full of good humor as the old one had been full of anxiety.

Old Frank looked as if he was whistling, Sidney had one arm aloft. Eileen was holding up her bouquet and blowing a kiss. Kate looked stunning. And Jasmin? Jasmin's face was wide open with anticipation. And, although she'd been standing straight-backed between her parents, the wind had whipped at her cotton dress in such a way that, once again, she looked as if she were carrying a child.

Jasmin studied the faces in the photo one by one. None of them, not even her own, seemed to belong to any world that she still knew. These are my people, she tried telling herself. But she knew that they weren't. Not any more. She would always love them, always care for them. But none of them could hurt her any more. And through them, at least, she could no longer hurt herself.

She looked up. Old Frank was already back inside the house. Kate and Eileen, small in the doorway, were fussing over the roses. She returned the photo to Sidney.

Do you want me to drive you back to Frank's now? she asked.

Sidney cocked his head. There is no rush, he said.

They began to walk, in step, toward the house. How did he persuade you to come here? she asked. What did he say that made you come?

Sidney looked at her, amused. Oh, nothing, he said. I had already made up my mind. I knew I had to come, really. I had to, for Kate. For everyone. So I was going to catch a bus. But then when I left the house, he was waiting there outside. And he offered me a lift.

But who did he say he was? asked Jasmin.

A friend of yours.

Nothing else?

Sidney shrugged. He said you had asked him to help. You know, to help the family.

Jasmin smiled and ushered her father ahead of her into the front garden. She looked back at the empty road.

He hasn't gone, she thought. Not really. He'll never really be gone.

250

42

I THINK, JASMIN SAID TO EILEEN, I THINK I'LL GO FOR A DRIVE. I'll go over and look at old Alice's grave.

As you wish, said Eileen, taking her by the arm and kissing her on the cheek. As you wish.

There was still an hour to kill before the Germans arrived. Jasmin needed to be away from the house. She needed to be on the outside. Shall I see if Sidney wants a lift now? she asked.

Eileen made no reply. She simply continued to look into Jasmin's face. Jasmin wetted her lips. She fished the keys out of her bag, and left on her own.

It was a short drive to the cemetery. She couldn't remember the geography of the place from the day of the funeral. So she had to find out at the gatehouse where Alice had been buried. She left the car outside the gates, and walked up the gentle slope. I'm pregnant, she told herself. And it's what I want. It is.

There was no stone yet, of course. Just a modest mound, several wreaths, and a marker. I should have brought flowers, thought Jasmin. She tugged up some of the longer grass in the area of the mound. Away over to the left, closer to the main road, a new grave was being dug.

Jasmin smoothed the skirt of her dress over her bottom and sat down next to where old Alice was buried. She pulled her knees up to her chin, linked her fingers across her shins, and stared down at the gatehouse, at her car, at the little road that stretched beyond. The wind had blown itself out, and now there was just a harmless breeze.

Through me he'll return, she thought. Through me he'll come again.

When she grew bored with the view, she opened her bag and took out Roland's book. She stared at the cover drawing of the baby Taliesin, floating among the salmon. Then she leafed through the story, rereading odd lines from the poems, smiling, nodding.

She put down the book. Such a little book.

She knew that she was waiting. But this wasn't the old kind of waiting. This was a time of growing, not wasting. In sitting still among those graves, listening to the traffic, she was taking all the initiatives that she needed to take.

She didn't have to wait for too long.

At first she didn't recognize the car, crawling up to the entrance, stopping behind her own. She knew that he couldn't see her. Not yet. She watched him slam his car door, make his enquiries at the gatehouse, then look up and scan the whole cemetery.

He made his way toward her at once. He was carrying flowers. Carnations by the look of them. Red, white, yellow. Lots of carnations. Jasmin had never felt such relief.

He strode closer in his inimitable way. The sun was making his glasses glint. He'll be here in a moment, thought Jasmin. He'll be here, and then in some different way it will go on. She unfastened her bag and put the book back inside.

Look, he called out when he was still some distance away, A peace offering! (He held up the bouquet.) I went to the house. Your mother told me you were here. Is it all right if I join you?

Jasmin put her hand to her brow, shielding her eyes from the sun's glare. He really looked as if he might go away if she said no. But she wanted him to stay. Now that she was safe, she was happy to be with him. He wasn't, after all, just any man.

I'd like you to have these, he said, proffering the carnations. It would be . . . better, if we could be friends.

Jasmin smiled, taking them. She held them, briefly, several inches from her face, then set them on the grass beside her. Roland took off his jacket, and sat down on the other side of the bouquet.

They both surveyed the view for a while without speaking. Roland unbuttoned his shirt cuffs and loosened his tie. Jasmin turned her head and gazed at him, the man who had said that he was available. The man who had volunteered—and had then been used for purposes which he couldn't begin to imagine. The man who was father, in every sense that didn't matter, to her unborn child.

What's up? he asked, apparently embarrassed by her close scrutiny.

Jasmin said nothing, but her eyes ranged all over his face, a good face, unknowing, a handsome face behind a beard.

Do you want me to go? he said. I'll go if you like.

Jasmin smiled at him lazily. I've behaved badly toward you, she said. It was wrong of me to try to lose you.

Roland looked away. Oh, he replied, You've just been having a hard time. I know what you've been going through . . .

Jasmin kept her eyes on him. He didn't know. He had no idea. And she no longer felt any need to tell him. She knew what she knew, and that was enough. That would always be enough. Roland's cheek was burning red. *There is nothing in which I have not been.* I'm going to have his baby, she thought. His.

Roland started to roll a cigarette. Jasmin reached out and kneaded the stem of a white carnation between her thumb and forefinger. What now? she asked him.

He looked down at her busy fingers, then into her eyes. I told you, he said. I'm there if you want me. If you need me. That's all.

Jasmin stared at the carnation stem. She wanted Roland already. She knew that she would need him.

He would be there. She would be there, too, for him.

And all around her, all the way out to the distant shimmering horizon and beyond, she could see the places where her protector had once walked—and would one day walk again.

She touched her stomach lightly before getting to her feet.

He's here, she thought. He's here.

Long and white are my fingers,
It is long since I was a herdsman.
I travelled over the earth
Before I became a learned person.
I have travelled, I have made a circuit,
I have slept in a hundred islands;
I have dwellt in a hundred cities.

Learned Druids,
Prophesy ye of Arthur?

Or is it me they celebrate?

Haydn Middleton was born in 1955 of an English mother and a Welsh father. He read Modern History at New College, Oxford, and has subsequently held jobs in advertising, publishing, and teaching. He now works as a free-lance writer, while also lecturing extramurally for Oxford University on British Mythology. Among his recent publications is *Son of Two Worlds*, an imaginative reconstruction of the fragments of a classic Celtic saga. He lives in Oxford with his wife and young family.